Fearfully, Anne stared at her bleeding hand.

Morgan reached beneath her, lifted her, and placed her safely away from the hay and its invisible weapon. "Let me see how bad you're cut."

"It's nothing," Anne said, keeping her hand close to her body. "I'm fine."

"You're not fine. You're bleeding. You may need stitches. Let me wipe it off and examine it."

Her eyes widened, reminding him of a deer trapped in headlights. "No! Don't touch it!"

"Why? I want to help. I've seen blood before."

"Stay away! Please, don't touch me." She was shaking all over.

"At least let me wrap my handkerchief around it to try to stop the bleeding." He fumbled in his jeans pocket.

"No!" She darted backward. "My father and I'll take care of it."

"But—"

"Please—you don't understand. I-I can't explain. Just don't touch it." Wild-eyed, panicked, she spun, and clutching her hand to her side, she bolted from the barn.

Dumbfounded, Morgan watched her run back toward her cabin.

ONE LAST WISH

Sixteen and Dying

BANTAM BOOKS
NEW YORK · TORONTO · LONDON · SYDNEY · AUCKLAND

RL 5, age 10 and up

SIXTEEN AND DYING

A Bantam Book / November 1992

The Starfire logo is a registered trademark of Bantam Books, a division of
Bantam Doubleday Dell Publishing Group, Inc. Registered in U.S. Patent
and Trademark Office and elsewhere.

ISBN 0-553-29932-8

Published simultaneously in the United States and Canada

Bantam Books are published by Bantam Books, a division of Bantam
Doubleday Dell Publishing Group, Inc. Its trademark, consisting of the
words "Bantam Books" and the portrayal of a rooster, is Registered in
U.S. Patent and Trademark Office and in other countries. Marca Regis-
trada. Bantam Books, 1540 Broadway, New York, New York 10036.

PRINTED IN THE UNITED STATES OF AMERICA

RAD 0 9 8 7 6 5 4

One

"ANNE, DOES THE ranch measure up?" her father eagerly asked.

Anne Wingate stopped unpacking and smiled. "Give me a minute, Dad. We just got here an hour ago."

Her father leaned against the four-poster bed where Anne had opened her suitcase. "Is your room as large as mine?" she asked. "Why don't you go unpack?"

"My room's fine. I'll unpack, but I want to be sure you're happy with everything first. No use staying if you don't like it."

Anne shook her head, controlling her urge to tell him to stop worrying so much. "The Broken Arrow Ranch seems to be just what the brochures promised," she said. "Wide open spaces, terrific luxurious cabins, and plenty of horses. Did you see how blue the sky is out here? The Rocky Mountains in the distance are awesome."

"Sure it's great, but I miss New York's skyscrapers!"

"Oh, Daddy, New York City isn't the only place in the world. I'm actually tired of concrete and smog, and of never seeing the sky. I've wanted to come to a place like this all my life. Remember, now that we're here, you promised to forget about the city and the university and everything back home. Start having a good time."

She wasn't angry. She knew her father only wanted her to be happy. Taking the summer off from classes as a history professor at New York University, closing up their apartment in Brooklyn Heights, and traveling out to Colorado to a dude ranch simply because she asked him hadn't been easy for him. Especially under the circumstances.

"If you have a good time, I'll have a good time," her father assured her. "You know I've only seen and ridden horses in Central Park, but I'll do my best." He watched her a few minutes longer, then asked, "Do you want anything? Can I help?"

"Dad, I'm sixteen. I think I can manage to unpack a suitcase by myself."

"I know, but it's been a long trip. I don't want you getting tired out."

Anne paused, observing her father. He was the one who looked tired. They had flown out of La Guardia at seven A.M., changed planes in Chicago, and landed in Denver. Now they were on Mountain Standard Time, but it was six o'clock in New York. Then, they'd been greeted by Tom Green, a representative from the Broken Arrow, and driven another hundred miles out to the ranch. Anne walked over to her father and put her hands on his chest. "Stop worrying about me. I feel just fine," she said softly.

"I can't help it. I—"

"You promised me we could have these few weeks to have a good time—just you and me."

"I know what I promised." Wearily, he raked his hand through his crop of fuzzy brown hair. "I'm a man of my word. I won't ask you any more questions."

Anne dropped her hands, glancing away, unable to tolerate the look of sadness on his face. She didn't want to be sad. She only wanted to finish unpacking and take a tour of the ranch. "Did you see the corral when we drove in? I want to walk down and get a look at the horses."

"I thought you were unpacking."

"There's plenty of time for that."

"Mr. Green said that dinner would be at six. You don't want to miss out on dinner in the mess hall."

"I'm sure I'll hear the dinner bell," Anne said. "Right now, I'm changing into jeans and going down to that corral."

Once she had changed, Anne left the small cabin she would be sharing with her father and hurried outside. She breathed the fresh, sweet-smelling air. She thought it was both wonderful and intoxicating.

Quickly, she got her bearings. She jogged past the cluster of cabins where the guests stayed, past the main lodge where guests and ranch hands shared meals, to a barn and a large corral where several horses milled about. Their hooves kicked up dust, making her cough. Anne boosted herself up onto the railing and peered over the top at the animals. She'd always loved horses, always wanted one of her own, but keeping a horse in the city was impractical. Over the years, she'd read books and collected pictures and horse figurines. She'd gone riding around Central Park, but that was never satisfying enough.

Anne held out her hand toward one of the horses. "Hey, fella," she called softly. The bay's ears pricked forward as she cooed to him. "Come on over. I won't hurt you." Anne wished she'd brought along a lump of sugar to tempt the animal closer.

"What do you think you're doing?"

The harsh male voice startled Anne, and she almost lost her balance on the fence. She half jumped, half fell the few feet to the ground and whirled to face an angry-sounding young man with broad square shoulders, black hair, and cold blue eyes. "Don't you know these premises are off-limits to you tourists?" He pushed his Stetson hat back on his head and gave her a withering look.

"I was just looking," Anne stammered, completely intimidated. The angry voice belonged to a handsome face. His denim shirt was soaked with perspiration, and his jeans looked dusty and well worn. He wore brown boots, caked with dirt and mud.

"These are range ponies," he added sharply. "They've been out on the range for months and have just been brought in. They're mostly wild. You could get hurt."

She didn't like being yelled at by someone who looked close to her own age. "I was being careful," she insisted. "I wasn't going to crawl over the fence, you know."

His blue eyes swept over her arrogantly.

"My dad and I got here about an hour ago from New York." Anne wasn't sure why she explaining anything to him, he was acting so unfriendly.

"Well, New York, the Broken Arrow is still a working ranch. The tourists' horses—the tame ones—are over in the other direction, on the far side of the cabins. You'll be safer petting one of them."

He made it sound like she was foolish—looking for a puppy to play with. Anne lifted her chin. "Well, Colorado, I'll use my compass next time so I can navigate to the other side of this place."

She saw his mouth twitch at the corners. He crossed his arms and held her gaze. "The name's not Colorado," he said. "It's Morgan."

"Like the breed of horse?" she asked.

He looked surprised that she could name a particular breed of horse. "That's right."

"Name fits you," Anne snapped. "Like the back end of the same." She spun and trooped off toward the cabins before her insult had time to register.

She hadn't gone far when he caught up with her. "We're responsible for visitors' safety," Morgan said, stepping in front of her, blocking her retreat. "An accident could cost us plenty in insurance."

She noticed that his tone didn't sound quite so condescending and that she'd become a "visitor" instead of a "tourist." "I didn't mean to go into a restricted area. I just got here. I guess I'll hear the guidelines tonight, so I won't get into the wrong place at the wrong time again."

Morgan stared at her until she began to grow uncomfortable, then asked, "What's your name?"

Anne wanted to ignore him, step around him, and return to her cabin. She didn't have much experience with boys, and he seemed unpleasant. "Why? Are you going to report me?" she asked.

His curious expression gave way as he sarcastically added, "Forget it, New York. I really don't care who you are. Just be careful. This isn't some spa—it's a real ranch, where people work. I wouldn't want you to chip a fingernail or something."

Anne watched him turn and march back toward the corral. She wanted to slug him. He was arrogant and rude, and she hadn't come more than a thousand miles to be insulted by some cocky cowboy. This was supposed to be her special summer with her father. A summer with no thought of what lay ahead for her.

She had selected the Broken Arrow after poring over dozens of brochures about dude ranches. The place seemed perfect. Why should she let a rude ranch hand ruin it for her? Anne turned her face skyward and took several deep breaths to calm her seething anger. The smell of hay and dust made her throat feel dry and parched, but was strangely exhilarating.

With a sigh, Anne welcomed the warmth of the sun on her skin, the feel of the breeze in her long, brown hair. Then, with a start, she realized that the beauty surrounding her, the quiet of the June afternoon, even the encounter with Morgan, had distracted her completely. Just for a little while, she had completely forgotten that she was dying.

Two

THE THOUGHT OF her problem left her shaken, as it always did, when it came upon her unexpectedly. *Dying.* That's what the doctors had told her in April. Anne walked slowly to the cabin but decided not to go inside yet. Her dad was probably taking a much needed rest. She sat down on the porch steps and watched the afternoon shadows grow longer, until shade covered her back and shoulders. Absently, she hooked her arms around her knees and allowed herself to remember. . . .

Nagging tiredness had drained Anne for months, no matter how much sleep she got. There were other problems too: her vision blurred while she was doing schoolwork, her appetite was poor, and she was losing weight. Eventually, her father noticed and insisted she get a checkup. A routine physical revealed nothing, but her family doctor suggested she have tests taken at the hospital.

Anne protested, but in the end, she spent spring break in St. Luke's Hospital while her friends went off on vacations. "We need to find out what's wrong," her father had said, trying to console her.

"But I'm missing all the fun!"

"We'll do something special this summer," he said.

Anne scoffed. "That's what you say every year, but then you end up teaching a summer course, and I end up taking enrichment classes."

"Anne, you should take extra classes. You're brilliant, and you'll qualify for a scholarship anywhere you want to go when the time comes. Don't worry about missing your break. I've already told the dean that you and I are going to be in Oxford next summer."

"Dad, England obviously has a lot to offer, but I'd prefer to go out West, someplace where there're horses and mountains and wide open spaces."

"Hang around smelly horses?" He feigned horror. "Wouldn't you rather walk along the Thames? Walk with Shakespeare, Wordsworth, Byron, and Shelley?"

Anne shared her father's love of books and had found comfort in poetry and novels ever since her mother's death, when she was ten. "You're not playing fair," Anne said, half pouting. "You know I look forward to going to England with you, but that's over a year from now. It seems like forever."

"The impatience of youth," her father kidded. "None of you kids can wait for anything. Trust me— next summer will be here before you know it."

Anne now looked back on that day and remembered it as the last carefree day of her life. That evening, Dr. Becksworth and Dr. Stevenson came into her room. She noticed their serious expressions. Her father, who was visiting with her, took her hand, as if to ward off their foreboding presence.

"Anne, we'd like to ask you some questions," Dr. Stevenson began without preamble. "They might sound odd, but it's important that you answer truthfully."

Wide-eyed, she glanced at her father, but nodded. "All right," she said, wondering why they'd think she might lie.

"Do you have a boyfriend?" Dr. Becksworth asked.

"No. I'm not really into dating." She felt color rise to her face. The question seemed completely off the subject. She didn't date at all. Not that she didn't want to, but the few boys who'd ever asked her out also attended her small private school, and she considered them boring and not really attractive. She'd rather not date at all than spend time with someone who didn't appeal to her.

"What's Anne's social life got to do with her medical problems?" her father asked. "Tell us the results of all those tests you've been running."

Dr. Becksworth gazed at Anne solemnly. "As a hematologist, I specialize in diseases of the blood."

Anne felt herself growing queasy. The idea that she might have some serious disease frightened her. "Do I have cancer?" she asked. She knew that leukemia was a blood disease.

"No," he said, giving her a momentary sense of

relief. "But according to your blood test results, you're HIV-positive."

Anne strained to make sense of his words and heard them echo in her head. "HIV-positive." She recalled that a famous athlete had announced that he was quitting pro basketball because he was HIV-positive. The announcement had shaken the country and caused a furor in her school. The administration and faculty had organized an awareness program about HIV and how it was transmitted, as if the kids didn't know already.

"Are you saying that my daughter has AIDS?" Anne's father demanded incredulously. "That's impossible! Absolutely impossible."

Anne was so taken aback that she couldn't speak.

"Please, Dr. Wingate," Dr. Becksworth said. "I'm not making any accusations. I'm simply trying to tell you what we've found and then figure out how Anne acquired the virus."

"I have AIDS?" Anne finally found her voice.

"No," Dr. Stevenson replied. "You have the virus that leads to AIDS." Anne couldn't sort out the distinction. The doctor continued, "I'm sure you know that AIDS is an immune-deficiency disease. The virus, HIV, attacks the body's T4 cells, which are the master programmers of the immune system. Without natural immunities, infections run rampant. Many illnesses are possible."

"According to your chart, you went to see a gynecologist a few weeks ago." Dr. Becksworth flipped through pages on a metal clipboard.

Anne felt her face redden. She gave her father a guilty, sidelong glance. "I didn't tell you, because it was . . . personal." Despite their closeness, there were some things Anne found difficult to share with her dad. If only her mother were still alive. She looked back at the doctor. "My gyn told me I had an infection and gave me some medicine."

"You still have the infection," Dr. Stevenson said. "The fact that it hasn't cleared up, combined with your other symptoms and blood results, is a signal of HIV."

"But Dr. Segal never said a word about that!"

"HIV is diagnosed only through a blood test. Very frankly, she would never have considered HIV in your case. There are other ways of getting this type of infection."

"I don't like your insinuations," Anne's father said quickly. "Your lab has messed up on my daughter's blood work. It's that simple."

Dr. Becksworth shook his head. "There's no mistake. I wish there were."

Anne felt tears stinging her eyes. "How could I have gotten HIV?" she asked. She felt trapped in some nightmare, caught in some awful, bad dream from which she couldn't wake up.

"That's what we must determine," Dr. Stevenson said kindly. "We need to figure this out, Anne, for everybody's sake."

"I don't know how," she cried. She felt her father's arm go around her protectively.

"You're not an intravenous drug user. Sharing contaminated needles is a major cause of transmission," Dr. Stevenson said. Anne shook her head emphatically. She never used drugs! "That's why I asked about your boyfriends," he said. "The virus is also sexually transmitted." Anne had a few friends who were having sexual relationships, but she certainly wasn't.

"Anne doesn't even date," her father said defensively.

Anne wished he'd keep quiet; he wasn't helping. The doctor put his hand on her shoulder. "If there was anyone, Anne, even if it was only once—"

Anne interrupted him. "No one. Not ever."

Dr. Becksworth cleared his throat. "The other most logical possibility is via a blood transfusion, but you said you haven't had one." He glanced back down at his chart.

"But, she has," Anne's father interrupted. "It was a long time ago, after the accident."

"When?"

The horror of the past flooded over Anne. "My mother and I were in an accident when I was ten. She died." Anne shook her head to dislodge the memories.

"Anne almost died too," her father added, holding her against his side. "They gave her a blood transfusion in the emergency room."

Anne scarcely remembered. She definitely recalled the long recuperation in the hospital. She and her dad, alone. Her mom, gone forever.

Dr. Becksworth nodded with understanding. "That was before eighty-five."

"It was in December. We were going Christmas shopping," Anne explained. The memory was extremely painful, even after almost seven years.

"It wasn't mandatory for labs to start screening blood for HIV until January eighty-five. All I can say is that it's very likely you received contaminated blood at that time."

Anne could scarcely absorb what the doctor was telling her. "But that was years ago!" her father exclaimed. "Why would it show up now?"

"One of the longest dormancy cases on record is almost ten years," Dr. Becksworth replied. "That's highly unusual, but Anne's young and healthy. Think back. Did she have any unusual complaints or symptoms in the first couple of weeks or even months after the transfusion?"

"My wife was dead, my daughter was in serious condition. How should I know?" her father snapped.

Anne touched his arm, stopping his explosion of temper. "Dad, I remember, I had a skin rash and my glands swelled up. The doctors thought I might be having a reaction to the antibiotic they were giving me."

"They should have caught it," her father stormed. "Why didn't they diagnose the virus then?"

"The test wasn't done routinely then," Dr. Stevenson explained. "There's no way that anyone would have guessed that someone in such a low-risk category as Anne might have contracted it. She was given the transfusion to save her life."

"I can't believe this is happening to me," she said suddenly, and her tears flowed freely. Blood—the very thing that once saved her life—was now turning her body against her.

"What are you going to do about it?" Her father challenged both doctors, balling his fist at his side.

"How are you going to keep my daughter from getting AIDS? How are you going to cure her?"

Dr. Stevenson took a deep breath and in a soft, troubled voice said, "I'm sorry. We'll do everything we can possibly do, but there is no cure for AIDS."

Three

$\backsim\!\!\heartsuit\!\!\sim$

"THERE ARE TREATMENTS —ways of delaying the onset, of stalling full-blown AIDS," Dr. Becksworth told them. "The drug AZT, especially combined with other drugs, is our most potent weapon in AIDS treatment at this time."

Anne wasn't concentrating on what he was saying. She felt as if she'd stepped out of her body and was standing at the side of the bed, hearing medical information about some stranger. It wasn't Anne they were discussing . . . it *couldn't* be. She was only sixteen. She had her whole life ahead of her. This was some terrible mistake. She felt shocked pity for the girl on the bed.

"I want a second opinion," Anne heard her father command.

She looked up at his face. It was the color of white chalk. "I think I need to be by myself for a while," Anne said softly. "I need to think about what you've told me."

"We can talk about it in the morning," Dr. Becksworth said. "The important thing is to start you on medication and begin a regimen for you before you leave the hospital."

"What about her day-to-day life?" her father asked, still agitated. "Is she supposed to drop out of school, stop going places?"

The idea of returning to school seized Anne, frightening her. How could she go back? What would happen when everyone found out she was HIV-positive? They'd hate her, shun her. Why, the administration might not even allow her to return!

"Anne should resume a normal life," Dr. Stevenson replied. "Once she starts taking AZT, and adjusts to its side effects, she can do the things she used to do."

"But the people I'm around—"

The doctor interrupted her. "The virus can't be passed through casual contact. Touching, kissing, even sharing eating utensils and drinking glasses won't spread the virus. Caregivers of AIDS patients do not contract the illness unless they exchange body fluids with the patients. We know for a fact that the virus isn't very strong outside the body—a simple disinfectant like chlorine bleach can destroy it. Don't worry about passing it to anyone, Anne. So long as you don't have sexual contact or donate blood, the people in your life are perfectly safe."

Anne wanted to laugh at him. *Perfectly safe.* Who was he kidding? The illness held such a stigma that no one was safe from the ostracism it caused. She wiped a tear aside.

When the doctors left, her father took her in his arms. His grip was so tight that she could hardly breathe. "I'll talk to other doctors," he promised. "There have got to be better doctors, specialists. We'll find someone to help you."

She felt sorry for him. She couldn't picture her father living alone. He needed her. They planned things together, cleaned their apartment together, did laundry together on Saturdays. She chose his ties and made certain he was on time for his classes. "Sure, Daddy. Whatever you say."

She finally made him go home, telling him she was exhausted. He swore to return first thing in the morning with other news. Once she was alone, Anne turned off the lamp and lay in the darkness. Only that morning, she'd thought she'd be home by now. Only hours before, she'd been annoyed at having to spend spring break in the hospital. How different her world looked now.

Her tears came as if a floodgate had opened. Why was this happening to her? What had she done to deserve such a terrible sentence as AIDS? First the loss of her mother, now the loss of herself.

She drifted off to sleep, but woke with a start, late in the night. She had the sensation that someone was in the room with her. Her heart pounded, yet as she glanced around, she saw that she was alone. Taking deep breaths to calm her ragged breathing, Anne turned her head. She noticed that beside her cheek, on her pillow, lay an envelope.

Curiosity beat out her fear. Anne flipped on the

light over her bed and squinted at the envelope. It looked like parchment and was sealed with wax, stamped with the initials OLW. Carefully, she broke the seal and pulled out two pieces of paper. One was a letter. She held it up to the light and began to read.

Dear Anne,

You don't know me, but I know about you, and because I do, I want to give you a special gift. Accompanying this letter is a certified check, my gift to you, with no strings attached, to spend on anything you want. No one knows about this gift except you, and you are free to tell anyone you want.

Who I am isn't really important, only that you and I have much in common. Through no fault of our own, we have endured pain and isolation and have spent many days in a hospital feeling lonely and scared. I hoped for a miracle, but most of all I hoped for someone to truly understand what I was going through.

I can't make you live longer. I can't stop you from hurting, but I can give you one wish, as someone did for me. My wish helped me find purpose, faith, and courage.

Friendship reaches beyond time, and the true miracle is in giving, not receiving. Use my gift to fulfill your wish.

Your Forever Friend,
JWC

Mystified, Anne looked at the check. It was made out to her in the sum of one hundred thousand dollars! She gasped. What was the One Last Wish Foundation? The check was signed by Richard Halloway, Esquire. Who would have done such a thing? She didn't know anyone with the initials JWC. She certainly didn't know anyone with so much money. Anne read the letter again and again. It said she could spend it on anything she wanted. Was one hundred thousand dollars enough to cure AIDS? She knew it wasn't. What good was money if it couldn't buy a future? She'd give the money to her father, if this was for real, at least he'd be able to be secure.

One hundred thousand dollars. She turned the possibilities for its use over in her mind. College? Probably not. Health care? How much did it cost to take care of someone with AIDS? Her funeral? Anne shook her head, hating the macabre direction her thoughts had taken. She decided to try to sleep. She'd wait until the morning and think about it again—if the check didn't evaporate. She put it under her pillow for safekeeping, turned out the light, and lay still in the dark.

Her father arrived while the nurses were clearing away the breakfast trays. His eyes were red-rimmed. He bent and kissed her. "You should have shaved, Dad. You look awful," she told him.

"I was up most of the night."

"Me too." She slipped her hand under her pillow to feel for the letter, certain she had dreamed it. The tip of her finger touched the edge of the envelope.

Her father sat down heavily in the chair next to

her bed. "I spent the night using the computer library looking for information about AIDS and the AZT treatment."

Anne's father had a modem, a special phone, on his home computer that tied into the university's system, so he could call up a data bank of reference libraries. She'd used it often when researching papers for school reports. "What's the bad word?" she asked.

"AZT is currently the best drug there is for AIDS treatment. There's also a drug called DDL, but people use AZT first."

"Tell me everything, Dad. Remember, I know how to use your computer, and can look this up for myself as soon as I get home, so save me the time and trouble."

He rubbed his eyes and slouched. "AZT's a powerful chemical. You'll have to take it several times a day and put up with the side effects—nausea, vomiting, tremors, depression."

"Sounds like a real lifesaver, all right."

"Patients adjust," he said, not hiding his sadness. "If things get too bad, you can go on antidepressants and other drugs to counter the effects."

Anne felt a fresh wave of tears clog her throat. It wasn't how she wanted to spend the last days of her life. "Is AZT my only choice?"

"It's your best choice."

"What if I don't start taking it right away?"

"What do you mean?"

"What if I wait until I actually get AIDS?"

"Anne, that's not wise. All reports suggest the importance of immediate treatment." Her father straightened and looked at her. "Doctors agree, the sooner, the better."

"What could be 'better' about being sick and depressed?" Anne felt herself getting angry, wanting to lash out at the shapeless enemy that waited to kill her. "You said there might be other doctors, specialists."

"I have the names of several specialists in the city."

"Maybe we should talk to one of them first."

"You mean, not go on the AZT immediately?"

"That's right. What difference could a few days make?"

He frowned, and Anne could see that her logic didn't appeal to him. "You're only putting off the inevitable."

"I don't care. I don't want to have to deal with this now. I want to go home, I want to finish the school term, and I don't want anyone to know about the diagnosis." She reached out to him. "We can keep it a secret, can't we, Daddy?"

"It's nobody's business," he replied. "We won't tell anyone until we have to. But we do need to see a specialist immediately. I don't think you should delay starting treatment for long."

Anne appreciated him for respecting her wishes, but then, he'd always treated her as an adult, capable of making her own decisions. "Please get me out of here," she said.

The doctors agreed to have her released that morning. At home, Anne tried to believe that life was normal, that she could pick up where she'd left off before her hospitalization. When her father had to go teach his classes, she set to work on the computer searching for information on AIDS treatment. She knew she was running up a large phone bill but figured it didn't matter. If the Wish money was for real, she could certainly pay a phone bill.

The more she studied, the more depressed she felt about her situation. All the treatments indicated debilitating side-effects, at least for awhile. She felt overwhelmed and immobilized by her situation. To divert herself, she reread the letter from JWC. The check was such an irresistible lure. *To spend on anything you want,* her benefactor had written. *Anything.*

In a burst of inspiration she turned to the computer bank libraries for information about ranches and summer vacations. Sometimes the descriptions were so vivid, she could almost smell the fresh mountain air. Ranch vacations offered horses, trail rides, grassy plains, and sun-drenched skies. For Anne, the ranches represented freedom. Choices.

When she realized what she wanted to do, Anne went to her father.

"Are you all right?" he asked anxiously when she asked to speak to him late one night.

"I feel pretty good considering." She sat down across from him in his study. "While I'm feeling so good, there's something I want to do." She handed him the letter. "First, read this. I think you're going to be as surprised as I was."

She watched as he read, his expression turning to utter amazement. Next, she handed him the check, which he examined closely. "It looks real," he said incredulously.

"I'm hoping it is real. Do you have any idea who

JWC can be? Maybe someone you or Mom once knew?"

"I haven't a clue. But it won't take long for me to validate the check's authenticity. I'll take it to the bank in the morning."

"If it's real, then I know what I want to do with it." She told him and he started shaking his head before she finished talking.

"I can't allow you to go play at a dude ranch this summer. You must begin treatments."

"I will take them, just not right away. All I want is a slight postponement, a reprieve. Let me have a few weeks of fun, then I'll start right in on the medication. I promise."

"Don't you know what you're asking? Your delay can accelerate the onset of AIDS."

Anne reached out and covered her father's hand with hers. "You've always allowed me to make my own choices. Please, Dad, let me have this one last wish. Please."

She saw him warring with his emotions and felt the full brunt of his anguish over giving her what she wanted. "Are you sure?" he asked.

"Very sure," Anne said. "It's my life, and it's what I want to do with it."

Four

ANNE WAS STARTLED by her father's voice as he pulled open the cabin door and stepped onto the porch. "Why are you sitting out here all alone?" he asked.

"I didn't want to wake you. Besides, it's beautiful outside, don't you think? Look at the sun setting behind the mountains."

Her father sat next to her on the steps. "My lungs aren't used to all this fresh air! It's going to take some adjusting. Were you able to get close to those smelly horses you like so much?" he asked.

His innocent question reminded Anne of her encounter with Morgan, the cowboy who'd taken an obvious dislike to her. She decided against telling her father about the rude way she'd been treated. "The horses were fine. There was one, a big bay, that I really liked."

"I thought a bay was a body of water."

"Oh, Dad, you're impossible! You're going to have a good time out here in spite of yourself. Wait and see. And thanks again for allowing me the grace period on taking the medication. This trip together means a lot, more than you'll ever know."

His grin faded, and he smoothed back her hair. "All I care about is your having a good time. Whenever I think—"

"Don't," she said. "Let's not depress ourselves."

They heard the clang of the dinner bell. She hopped up and dusted off the seat of her jeans. "Saved by the bell. I'm hungry. How about you?"

"Starved." He stood up, and together they walked the distance to the rustic-looking lodge. They were joined by other guests in a huge main room, sectioned off into more intimate areas by the furniture arrangement. Along one wall there was a massive stone fireplace, which Anne imagined could be cozy when the winter wind howled outside. The scent of fresh pine mingled with the smells of pot roast and warm bread coming from a long wooden table set with dinner plates and steaming bowls of food at the opposite end of the room.

"Come on! Don't be shy," said a tall, brown-haired woman from the head of the table. "Welcome to the Broken Arrow. If you don't hustle up to the dinner table, my boys will clear it off like a plague of locusts."

Anne saw a line of cowboys standing behind chairs at the table. She could tell they were workers by the weathered look of their clothes. The guests stood out in their brand-new jeans and store-pressed shirts. Even though her own jeans weren't new, they had a designer chic about them.

"Take a chair anyplace," the woman said. "My name's Maggie Donaldson. My husband, Don, and I own this ranch, and we want you to have a fine old time while you're with us." A large man with sun-weathered features stepped up beside Maggie and waved.

Anne and her father chose chairs about midway down the table. She glanced about curiously, hoping to see girls her age, though many of the guests seemed to be couples with young children.

Anne shook out her dinner napkin and placed it across her lap as Maggie continued with introductions. "These kids will be our waiters." She motioned to a cluster of young people who emerged from the kitchen. "Many are college and high school kids from all over the country who've come here to work, earn some money, and have a taste of the West. They'll be responsible for cooking, clean-up, cabin clean-up—in short, whatever you need to make your visit to the Broken Arrow the best. And the ranch hands are here to work, but if you need anything, ask one of them. We all want to help."

Maggie gestured toward the food. "Right now, eat up. We'll have a meeting later tonight to tell you what's in the works for you all this week. The hands get up early, and you will too. There's too much to do for a body to lie abed all day."

Once Maggie had completed her speech, the bowls of hot foot were passed along the table. A girl who Anne guessed was close to her in age came alongside with a basket of hot rolls. Anne smiled, and she smiled back and moved on.

Morgan Lancaster watched Anne from the other side of the table, warily. He was convinced that he knew her type—pretty, rich, and pampered. It was the only part of life on the ranch he hated. Every summer, his Aunt Maggie and Uncle Don took in wealthy, often snobby guests who thought that a few weeks on a ranch made them experts on the West.

The spoiled teenage girls were the worst, to his way of thinking. Some of them had provided diverting summer fun for him over the years, but for the most part, he didn't like them. And he didn't like the girl across the table from New York City, either. The only thing that got to him about her was her large, expressive brown eyes, which appeared somehow sad. What could a rich girl from the East have to be sad about? He could tell her plenty about sadness, if he had a mind to. *Forget it,* he told himself. She wasn't worth his time.

Aunt Maggie stood up and clanged her spoon against the side of her water glass. "When you're finished, feel free to wander around the premises. Stables for the horses and ponies you'll be assigned to ride during your stay are open for you to tour. Our boys will be glad to show you around. There'll be a roping demonstration down at corral four—maps are available at the desk. Remember, the lodge never closes, so come over anytime, day or night. See you back here at eight for the general meeting."

"So, what do you think?" Anne asked as she and her father walked toward their cabin after dinner.

"I think the food's great, but I don't know about

all this fun stuff. Frankly, I'm glad I brought along my laptop computer."

"You're impossible!" Anne exclaimed, hooking her arm through his. "I'm going down to the stables to choose my horse for the trail ride tomorrow."

"You do that," her father said. "I'll see you back at the lodge for the meeting. I'm glad to see you smiling so much."

Anne threaded her way around the cabins. She heard the sound of children laughing. The softness of the summer night, the laughter and squeals, made her pause. She would never hear the sound of her own children. Melancholia stole over her. The thought jarred her. Until now, she'd never even thought about being married and having children.

Even if the AZT helped her body arrest the inevitable progress of AIDS, having children was out of the question. The virus could be passed to a pregnant woman's unborn baby. Anne knew she couldn't do that to an innocent baby. *No marriage. No babies. No sex.* Anne mentally went down the list of what HIV was denying her.

"Stop thinking about it," Anne told herself firmly. No sex didn't mean no love. She told herself there was a difference, but what man would want to love her, knowing he couldn't have a total relationship with her?

The Wish money had offered her a few weeks of uninterrupted happiness. She wanted to capture all the fun and good times she could for whatever time she had left. She forced herself to resist negative thoughts about tomorrow, and concentrate on the here and now.

She was just rounding the final cabin site when she heard the distinct sound of someone crying. Anne stopped and strained to catch the direction of the soft sobs, then started toward the source.

For a moment, Anne studied the girl who'd served the rolls at dinner. She tried to put herself in the girl's place. Would she want some nosy stranger to intrude on her sadness? Yet, even as she wondered, Anne knew she would speak. "Excuse me," Anne said. "Can I help?"

The girl started, wiped her eyes, and turned away. "*Nada*," she said in Spanish. "Nothing."

"I have a friend back in New York," Anne told her. "Whenever she says 'it's nothing,' she means 'it's the end of the world.' I won't pry, but if there's anything I can do . . . even just listen . . . I will."

With her back still turned, the girl said nothing. After a few awkward moments, Anne stepped backward. Admonishing herself for interfering, Anne started to leave.

She'd gone only a few steps when she heard the girl's quivering voice say, "Don't go . . . please. I need to talk to someone. I'm so unhappy, I could die. Just die."

Five

A SLIVER OF MOONLIGHT allowed Anne to see the girl's tear-streaked face. "I'm Anne Wingate. What's your name?"

"I'm Martes Rodriguez—my friends back home in Los Angeles call me Marti. You're obviously a guest here. I *have to* spend the summer out here working. My parents are forcing me."

"They're making you work here against your will?"

"It's really all my brother's fault. Luis is a cop in L.A. He's the one who arranged to have me sent out here. About ten years ago, he worked here for two summers in a row. He said it saved his life, because he was in a gang and now all the boys from that gang are dead. He'd be dead too, he said, if it hadn't been for this place and the Donaldsons' influence. According to him, this place turned his life around." Marti sounded angry.

"You're in a gang?" Anne could scarcely believe that the trim, raven-haired girl in front of her ran with a street gang.

"Not me. My boyfriend, Peter Manterra. My family thinks he's bad for me. What do they know? They don't remember what it's like to be in love."

Anne saw that Marti was hurting, but she couldn't imagine feeling such sorrow over being separated from a boyfriend. "It's only for a summer. Maybe time will pass more quickly if you're busy."

"I doubt it. Did you leave a guy back home?"

"Not me. I wanted to spend the summer here. I'm with my father. He's the only guy in my life! I thought a summer out West on a ranch sounded like fun."

Marti made a face. "I don't mind the work, but I miss Peter so much. What if he finds another girlfriend? What if he forgets about me?"

"But if he really loves you, why would he look for another girl?"

"You sound like my mother," Marti retorted.

Anne laughed. "I'm sorry. I guess that was a parent-type thing to say. But the way you're complaining about being here reminds me of my father. He gripes constantly about the fresh air and open spaces."

Marti smiled tentatively. "I didn't mean to complain about the ranch. Actually, I think it's a pretty nice place. I live in L.A. near the barrio, and summers are hot and mean. I guess that in some ways, this is a change for the better." She cut her eyes sideways. "*Un pocito.* That's Spanish for a '*very* little.' "

"You can write to your boyfriend, can't you? Every day if you want to."

"I guess, but it's hard being separated from him. I love him so much. You must know what it's like." Anne didn't want to admit that she had no idea what it felt like to be in love. "Why are you here just with your dad?" Marti asked, blowing her nose. "Are your parents divorced?"

"My mother died years ago. It's just me and my dad. I'm used to it, I guess." Then, changing the subject, she asked, "Will you get to go on any trail rides with us? Maybe riding horses can take your mind off your boyfriend."

"The workers are kept pretty busy. We got here over a week before you guests arrived. Our free time's our own whenever we can grab some of it. I hope to do a lot more riding. A couple of the hands, some of the younger guys, have offered to take me along. The owners' nephew, Morgan, works on the ranch like an ordinary hired hand, and he's been nice to me," Marti added.

Morgan's image sprang into Anne's mind. "What's so unusual about that?"

"You can bet that if I were related to the owner, I wouldn't be working like a hired hand." She paused thoughtfully. "But you know, he's a regular person, not bossy or mean one bit. He's kind of reckless though. He reminds me of my brother, Luis . . . kind of *loco*, you know, crazy." Marti made a face. "But if it weren't for Morgan and his friend, Skip, I'd have gone crazy last week."

Anne could hardly believe that Marti was describing the same guy she'd had words with at the corral. "You sure Morgan was really nice?" she said.

"What do you mean?"

"Nothing, forget it." Anne peered at Marti more closely. Her tears had completely dried. "Feeling better?"

Marti nodded. "Thanks. I guess I really did need to talk to someone—someone female and my age who'd understand."

"Since we're both going to be here for the summer, maybe we can do things together," Anne offered. Although Marti was different from Anne's friends in New York, Anne already liked her. She was open and honest about her feelings.

"I'd like that. The other girls working with me are older—sophomores and juniors in college. We don't have much in common. I could use a friend. My quarters are on the south side of the lodge, in cabins close by the kitchen. Maybe we could meet tomorrow afternoon. I have free time from two till four."

Anne gave Marti her cabin number and invited her to come by anytime. The crunch of boots on gravel made them both turn. Morgan ignored Anne and addressed Marti. "My aunt's looking for you. They've cranked some ice cream, and she wants you to help serve it after the meeting."

"Back to the salt mines." Marti sighed and shrugged. "See you around, okay? I'm glad we got to talk."

Anne watched her hurry off. Alone with Morgan, she felt unsure of herself. "I was headed to the stables, toward the *tame* horses," she said, unable to resist getting in a dig. "I heard Marti crying and investigated."

Morgan hooked his thumbs through the belt loops of his jeans. "Marti's all right—sort of lost out here, but she's getting used to it. My buddy, Skip, has taken a liking to her."

Anne wasn't sure why it pleased her to know that Skip, not Morgan, was interested in Marti. "I guess I'll get down to the stables before all the decent horses are snatched up."

"Would you like me to help you pick a mount?" Morgan's offer surprised Anne. He continued quickly, "I know the animals—all their idiosyncrasies. I could help you choose the right one."

"Yes, I'd appreciate your help," she said. His input could be valuable. She wanted a horse with some spirit.

As they walked to the stable in silence, Morgan wondered why he'd volunteered. Yesterday, he'd decided to steer clear of this particular girl, and now he was headed to the stables with her. Deep down, he felt Anne of New York City was trouble. She obviously had money and probably was spoiled. He thought back two summers before, when he'd been sixteen and fallen like a load of bricks for Stacy Donner, a rich debutante from San Francisco. She'd toyed with him. He learned from the experience. Rich girls were fickle and not to be trusted.

At the stable, Anne stopped in front of each stall and studied each horse. The horses were well cared for and content. "Most are quarter horses," Morgan explained. "They've worked on the range and earned the right to some leisure time."

"Not like the ones in the other corral," Anne said. "I liked them better."

"They're wild. Most of them are jugheads."

"Jugheads?"

"That's what we call a horse with no sense. They usually end up as broncos in rodeos."

"The bay seemed different."

Her natural eye for horseflesh impressed Morgan. "I'm going to cut him out and work with him. I'd like a new horse, but first I've got to see if it's worth the time and effort to train him."

"You mean you're going to break him yourself?" The idea of taming and training a wild horse fascinated her.

"It's no picnic. It's hard, time-consuming work," Morgan replied. He pushed back the brim of his hat and gazed down at Anne. "Before I make a recommendation about a horse, why don't you tell me which one you think is right for you."

Anne wandered back along the stalls. She stopped in front of a good-size palomino. "If I have a choice, I'll pick this one. He's got nice confirmation and bright eyes."

Morgan was pleased. Anne had chosen the horse he would have picked for her. "That's Golden Star, a nine-year-old gelding. He's yours while you're here."

Anne smiled. "I've always wanted to have my own horse—and now I will, even if it is only temporary." *Temporary.* Now, everything about her life was temporary. She wondered if JWC, her mysterious benefactor, had experienced this sense of impermanence.

"Making plans too far into the future is stupid,"

Morgan said. "You never know what's going to come along and blow them away."

Anne was surprised that he seemed to understand a person's life could be shot down, even when the person did nothing to bring it about.

"Look, I should get back to the lodge. Do you mind?" he asked.

"No problem. I'll stay here and admire my new horse, then head back for ice cream." She was glad he was being nicer.

Anne watched him walk away and tried not to feel so hopeless. This ranch represented everything she could never have, everything that had been stolen from her by an unalterable circumstance. Tears welled in her eyes and slid softly down her cheeks.

Six

ANNE AWOKE BEFORE dawn the next morning. She tossed restlessly, finally got up, dressed, and headed down to the main lodge. Maggie Donaldson glanced up. "Morning," Maggie said with a broad, friendly smile. "You're up early."

"Couldn't sleep."

"You'll be so tired by this time tomorrow, we'll have to shake you awake."

Anne saw some of the kitchen crew clearing away the table. "Did I miss breakfast?"

"The hands eat early so they can be about their chores. But you've got a few hours before the morning bell. Would you like a piece of fruit to hold you over?"

Anne plucked an apple from a fruit bowl on the table and waved at Marti, who offered a smile and exaggerated sigh. "Catch you later," Marti said.

Anne wandered over to where Maggie was working. "I already like the ranch," she told her. "I've lived in New York City all my life. It's so different out here."

"I'll bet." Maggie's kind green eyes looked up at Anne. "I grew up out here—my Pa, Frank Lancaster, owned the next spread over. I married Don, who owned this place, and when it became impossible to make ends meet ranching alone, we decided to open the place up in the summer. Guests get a taste of the West, and we get to keep working the ranch."

"You've never traveled out of Colorado?" she asked.

"Oh, I've been to other places, but no place I liked better."

"Do you have family here too?"

"Just Morgan, my brother's boy."

Anne was curious about why Morgan wasn't with his father. She would have thought the families would be working together. "Where's your brother?"

Maggie looked up, catching Anne's gaze and holding it. She said nothing, and Anne knew that she'd overstepped the boundary of small talk. Just as Anne began to feel self-conscious, Maggie said, "Why's a pretty little girl like you sitting around jawing with an old gal like me? You should go out into that fresh air and watch the sun come up. It's a pretty sight you'll never forget."

"Sometimes entire days go by and we don't see the sun in New York City." Anne laughed.

"Then all the more reason to see the sun come up over God's country. When you hear that morning bell, come back for flapjacks and bacon."

Anne walked outside. She realized Maggie had definitely changed the subject when she'd asked about Morgan's father. She shrugged. It wasn't any of her business anyway. Just as her life wasn't any of theirs.

Overhead, the sky was turning gray with faint streaks of yellow and pink. She heard the sounds of men's voices, hollering and whooping. Curious, she followed the noise and soon found herself near the corral she'd discovered the day before. A group of men hung over the fence watching. Anne edged closer, straining to see what the commotion was about.

"Come on, Morgan, show him who's boss," a dark-haired man called.

"He's ornery, but you can take him," another fellow shouted.

Anne unobtrusively slipped into an opening in the cluster of men. In the center of the corral, she saw Morgan standing in front of the big bay range horse. The horse was blindfolded and held by a taut rope around its neck. Morgan, holding the rope, was attempting to inch closer, all the while muttering soothing words to calm the frightened animal.

One of the men called out, "You can think of plenty of sweet things to say if you pretend it's a pretty woman."

The hands laughed, and Morgan retorted, "How would you know, Ben? The last pretty woman you talked to fainted dead away."

Catcalls followed. Anne grasped the fence and leaned against the rough wood. She saw Morgan gather the rope tighter, until he was almost nose to nose with the horse. He ran his gloved hand along the bay's tense neck and said, "Take it easy, boy. I won't hurt you."

Anne watched as Morgan retrieved a bridle that dangled from the back pocket of his jeans. Expertly, he slipped the bit between the animal's teeth. The horse protested, half rearing. Anne gasped, as she saw the hooves strike the air near Morgan's head. Morgan maintained control with the rope, using his strength to force the bay down. Dirt flew from the horse's hooves. The men shouted more encouragement.

Tossing the reins over the horse's shoulders, Morgan stepped to one side and, catlike, sprang onto the bay's broad bare back. A cheer went up. In the gathering light of dawn, Anne could make out the tenseness of the horse's muscles. They looked like springs waiting to uncoil.

"Here goes nothing," Morgan announced. He leaned forward and whipped the bandanna off the horse's eyes. The bay struggled to dip his head and then exploded into a bucking, twisting banshee.

Morgan stayed with the horse for what Anne thought was a long time. Then, the horse flung him off, and Morgan flipped through the air and hit the ground hard on the far side of the corral. She squealed in spite of herself.

The minute the horse was relieved of his burden, he stopped bucking and began to gallop around the ring. Morgan scrambled for safety. Hands reached through the bars of the fence as the horse thundered past, and Morgan was pulled to safety. "You all right?"

Gingerly, Morgan dusted himself off. "Sure. . . . That was some ride."

"What's going on?" A man's voice bellowed. Anne spun to see Morgan's uncle charging toward the corral like an angry bull. "You get to your chores!" he commanded. The men slunk away.

Anne tried to vanish but was trapped by the wall of the barn. She hid in its shadows while Morgan's uncle continued, "Not you, Morgan. You stay put."

Anne saw Morgan bend, pick up his hat, and stand to face his uncle, squaring his shoulders in defiance. "What is it, Uncle Don?"

"What do you think you're doing? Are you crazy?"

"Breaking in the horse. You said I could have my pick of the range ponies, and that's the one I want."

"You know how to break a horse proper. You break him to saddle first. *Then* you climb on. You could have gotten killed out there."

"So what?"

"Don't take that tone with me. Maggie would never get over it if anything happened to you."

"Something could happen to me no matter how careful I am. Her too. You know what I mean."

"No one can see the future, and you don't know anything for sure," Uncle Don said angrily. "I won't have you taking needless chances while you're on my spread and under my care."

"I'm eighteen. I can come and go whenever I want."

"You go and you'll break your aunt's heart." Uncle Don ran his hand through his close-cropped hair and released a heavy sigh, his anger spent. "I don't want to argue with you, son, but I have a ranch to run. It might be your ranch someday. I can't let my hands defy me—not even you, no matter if you are family. I have rules, and I expect them to be followed. If that's the horse you want, you've got him, but you break him right. Fair enough?"

Morgan shoved his hands into his pockets. "Fair enough," he agreed.

"I need you to ride out and check fencing today. Can you handle that?"

"I can handle it."

Anne sensed a thick tension coming from Morgan. She held her breath and hugged the wall tighter. If either of them caught her eavesdropping, she'd be embarrassed to death. She hadn't meant to listen but now that she had, she found Morgan more intriguing than ever.

She couldn't help wondering if one summer would be enough time for her to figure him out. One summer. It was all she had.

Seven

By THE END of the day, Anne realized Maggie hadn't exaggerated about how tired she'd be. She stifled a yawn at the dinner table. "Maybe you're overdoing the outdoors routine," her father suggested anxiously. "Maybe you should take it easy, rest more."

Anne didn't bother to argue with him. "What do you know about the outdoors? While the rest of us went on a trail ride, you sat in the cabin with your eyes glued to your computer screen."

"I'm doing a paper for a journal on medieval lifestyles. I have a deadline to meet," he said. "I'm sure there'll be another ride tomorrow."

"Will you make that one?"

"Would you miss me if I skipped it?"

Anne hugged him to answer.

That night, when everyone settled around a large

campfire to hear a cowboy tell tall tales, Marti
slipped in beside Anne. "Having fun?" she asked.

"Yes, but I ache all over."

"That's normal. After my first day on a horse, my
buns were so sore, I could hardly stand."

Anne smiled. She didn't say that she'd ridden often in Central Park on horses she rented. Of course,
at the time, she'd ridden hunt seat on English-style
saddles, which was different from the wider western
saddle style, but the same part of her anatomy was
involved. "I enjoyed the trail ride," Anne said. "I
wish you could have come along."

Marti picked up a stick and drew circles in the
dirt. "Skip wants me to ride out somewhere with
him and have a picnic."

"You don't sound very enthusiastic. I've seen
Skip—he's cute."

"I don't think I should."

"Why not?"

"Actually, I think Skip's cute, too, and he's really
nice to me. But if I really love Peter, then I shouldn't
be attracted to Skip, should I?"

Anne watched Marti nibble nervously on her
lower lip. "Why not? You're not engaged to Peter,
and you think he might date other girls this summer. Why shouldn't you date Skip? Isn't this one of
the reasons you're out here—to see if your relationship with Peter is the real thing? I mean, if he loves
you, and you love him, then dating others shouldn't
make a difference in your feelings toward each
other, should it?"

Marti was looking at her, wide-eyed. "What you're
saying makes sense. I like Skip as a companion. I'd

like to get to have some fun. It's nothing serious. Plain fun." She perked up. "I have an idea. Why don't you come along on the picnic?"

"I'm certain Skip wants me as a chaperon!"

"No, no, silly. His friend, Morgan, can come too."

"Oh, I don't think—"

"You could do worse than Morgan." Marti batted her dark lashes as she pleaded with Anne. "As a favor for your *amiga*. That's me. Your friend. *Por favor*?"

Anne giggled. It was hard to say no to Marti. Anne couldn't deny that she was drawn to the idea of spending time with Morgan. She wanted so much to have a good time, but she felt as if she were trying to live two lives. One, as a regular sixteen-year-old. The other, as a sixteen-year-old stricken with HIV, who had nothing in front of her but a lingering death once full-blown AIDS hit. How could she make it with so much bottled up inside her? With no one to talk to? Is that what JWC had meant by saying, *"I hoped for a miracle, but most of all I hoped for someone to truly understand what I was going through."*

"Are you okay?" Marti asked. "You checked out on me for a minute."

"Sorry. All this talk about romance made me hyperventilate," she quipped, to hide what she couldn't reveal. "Don't worry. I've got it under control now."

Marti burst out laughing. "Anne, you're so funny! I'll bet you're the life of the party at your school."

"That's me—party girl."

"Then it's settled," Marti said. "I'll tell Skip you're coming on our picnic, and he'll tell Morgan. We're going to have so much fun, Anne. Wait and see. A real *fiesta*."

Anne figured that Morgan would probably nix the whole idea. Marti tossed the stick into the campfire, and Anne, deep in thought, watched the flames devour it.

At the end of the first week, Anne's father informed her, "I've made an appointment this coming Monday with Dr. Rinaldi, the specialist you're supposed to see here. I've asked Maggie Donaldson if I can use the station wagon to drive you into Denver."

"Dad, how could you? I don't want to see a doctor. Besides, Monday is another trail ride, and I don't want to miss it."

"Anne, this isn't up for debate. You have to be evaluated. You must stay on top of your medical condition as long as you're in Colorado."

"Well, I hate it, and I don't want to think about it."

"It's not going to go away."

"I, of all people, know it's not going away." The pain in his eyes made her sorry she'd lashed out at him. "All right," she said, feeling remorseful. "I'll go. But I don't have to like it."

They left the ranch right after breakfast and drove the hundred miles to Denver. The city, with traffic and noise and exhaust fumes everywhere, was a shock to her senses. The weather was dry and hot, made hotter by the sun's reflecting off concrete and glass buildings. The large hospital complex was surrounded by looping roads and expansive asphalt parking lots, packed with parked cars. Anne missed the quiet ranch.

She endured the blood test and physical, then sat with her dad in Dr. Rinaldi's office while the physician reviewed her records.

"How's Anne doing?" Her father craned his neck to see the chart the doctor held.

"Her lungs are clear. However, she's anemic, so I want her taking iron and B-12 to build up her red blood count."

"Maybe that's why I'm feeling tired," Anne offered.

"You've been bothered by fatigue?" her father asked. "You didn't tell me."

"It's no big deal, Dad."

"Yes, it is a big deal," Dr. Rinaldi countered. "Fortunately, your T4 cell count is still up around five hundred. If it falls below two hundred, you're going to be at serious risk for infections. That patch of dry, flaky skin on your back and upper legs is also a symptom of lowered T cells. I'll give you a cream for the rash."

Anne only nodded. The information about her T4 cells bothered her. While the number was still within acceptable limits, it was lower than when she left New York. She felt time and good health slipping away from her. "I'll do what you tell me," she promised.

"I've spoken with Dr. Becksworth in New York, Anne," Dr. Rinaldi said. "We both think it prudent that you start on AZT right away."

She still didn't want to. She didn't want to face the side effects. She'd made so many plans with

Marti and Morgan. "Please let me have three more weeks at the ranch. As soon as I get back home, I'll begin taking the drug."

"I don't think that's wise," Dr. Rinaldi replied.

"You don't understand," she insisted. "I need to live normally before I die." She felt waves of desperation.

"Anne, be reasonable," her father said. "It's your life."

"Don't force me to do this yet," she begged.

"I understand how you feel, but I disagree," Dr. Rinaldi said. "Nevertheless, I can't force you to start on AZT against your will. However, if you have any new symptoms—fever, shortness of breath, or persistent cough—I want you right back here to start the medication. Understand? The length of time from infection with HIV to the development of AIDS hasn't been adequately researched in women. All we kow for certain is that women face serious illnesses with AIDS that men don't, for instance, cervical cancer and pulmonary tuberculosis."

"If you're trying to scare me, Dr. Rinaldi, it's working," Anne said. Her hands felt cold and clammy, and she was getting queasy.

The doctor's gaze softened.

"I know you want me to begin treatment, and I'm being stubborn," Anne told him. "I'm not in denial. I know I have HIV. I've had to accept other things I couldn't control—like my mother dying. It's made me tough."

Dr. Rinaldi steepled his fingers. "Women with AIDS are dying six times faster than men with AIDS. Once a woman is diagnosed with AIDS, her life expectancy is less than thirty weeks. I simply want to delay that time for you as long as possible, Anne."

"Listen to the doctor," her dad pleaded. "Let's go back to New York or start on the AZT, Anne."

"People can beat odds," Anne said, lifting her trembling chin. "Dad, let me have a few more weeks to remember."

"All I can help you with is postponement of full-blown AIDS," the doctor replied. "AZT has the power to delay the onset."

"But not the inevitable," Anne remarked.

"No, not the inevitable."

She looked from Dr. Rinaldi to her father. She felt their anguish on her behalf, yet she couldn't forget why she'd come to Colorado. JWC had given her the Wish money without strings, to spend on anything she wanted. Anne knew what she wanted. "Then, if the outcome is exactly the same either way, I'd rather have a few weeks of freedom. I can't forget what's hanging over my head, and I know you're both only trying to help me. . . . Thank you for that. I have very few choices for my life. Please, let me make this one."

Morgan paused while walking the bay stallion around the training ring when he saw the station wagon coming up the long drive toward the main lodge. Anne and her father had been in Denver the whole day. *Probably shopping*, he thought. His mother used to shop continually. Even when there was no money.

He watched the car pull into its parking space and Anne and her father get out. Even from his distance,

Morgan could see how exhausted and defeated they appeared. Anne's father tucked her under his arm as they headed toward their cabin. To Morgan, the gesture appeared protective.

Morgan thought of Anne as beautiful and wealthy. What in the world could she have to be unhappy about? He pulled the tether and clicked to the horse. The horse obeyed, following Morgan docilely as he resumed walking in the ring.

"I need to stop thinking about that girl," he told the bay. Yet, even as he said it, Morgan knew it was becoming impossible to do so. Somehow, Anne and her sad eyes had gotten under his skin. Which was stupid—especially in his case, when he knew what his own future might hold. Exceedingly stupid.

Eight

MORGAN BEGAN TO watch Anne. He observed that although she joined in many of the group activities, every afternoon she saddled up Golden Star and rode off alone. One afternoon, curiosity got the better of him, and he followed her.

He allowed Anne plenty of distance. Since he was an expert tracker, he easily picked up her trail if she got too far ahead. He figured out that she was heading toward Platte City, a small town about ten miles north of the Broken Arrow. Many of the married ranch hands lived there with their families, and sometimes Morgan went to the town to relieve the monotony of ranch life. The main street offered residents only a few stores, a movie theater, an ice-cream parlor, and a pizzeria. He couldn't figure out what Anne found to do there every day.

He rode up on the outskirts and reined in his

horse. He saw Golden Star tied to a tree in the yard of the local church. The whitewashed wooden building was very old, but in good repair. Its tall steeple stabbed into the sky, and from the looks of the parking lot, the church appeared deserted. Morgan dismounted, tied his horse to the tree, and slowly climbed the front steps. As he reached for the door handle, he lost his nerve. What would she think if she saw him come inside?

"Just don't let her see you," he told himself, pulling open the door. Inside, sunlight slanted through a single stained-glass window, spilling a rainbow of colors over the altar. The wooden floor and pews gleamed, and a faint odor of lemon wax hung in the quiet air. He saw Anne sitting alone in the very last pew, her head hung low. Suddenly, he felt like a trespasser. He tried to ease out, but his boot scraped on the floor, and she turned.

Her eyes grew wide with recognition. "What are you doing here?" she asked, looking as if he'd caught her doing something sinful.

"I saw Golden Star tied outside, and I came in to investigate." He hoped the half-truth would be enough of an explanation for her. "You okay?"

"Sure. Fine. I was . . . um . . . just contemplating."

"Contemplating what?"

"Things." She gestured vaguely. "I asked permission from the minister. He said I could stay."

"I'm not prying," Morgan said hastily. Now that the mystery was solved, he felt foolish. "I was surprised to see one of the ranch's horses outside . . . that's all."

Anne stood. "I come here some afternoons to be

alone. Some days, I stop by the library and check out books. I'm real careful with the horse."

"I'm not worried. I've seen how well you take care of him." He fiddled with the hat he'd removed when he came inside. "You go to the library? Man, when I graduated, I swore I'd never read another book." Anne looked horrified, as if he'd blasphemed. He chuckled. "Let me guess. You're a bookworm."

"The worst kind. I can't imagine never reading another book. It would be like your never riding another horse." She started for the door, and he felt bad, sensing he had spoiled something special for her.

"I didn't mean to interrupt you."

"It's all right." She glanced at her watch. "I should be heading back, before Dad misses me."

He followed her outside, where they paused and blinked against the brightness of the sun. To one side of the church, there was an old cemetery. "Have you ever checked out the tombstones?" he asked, trying to make up for intruding on her. "Some of them date back a hundred years."

For a moment, her expression clouded, then her large brown eyes warmed. "Show me," she said.

He walked her through the old graveyard, pointing to various headstones. He stopped at one and said, "Here lies my Great-great-great Grandmother. She was a full-blooded Cheyenne who converted to Christianity." The stone looked ancient and sunbleached and bore the name Woman Who Wears a Cross.

"I didn't realize your family went back so far. Tell me about them."

Morgan was annoyed at himself for mentioning it. The last thing he wanted to discuss was his family. "Some other time," he said, stepping to the next marker.

Anne stooped and plucked a handful of wildflowers from around the old gravestone. "One of my favorite poets is Emily Dickinson. She wrote about death in many of her poems." Anne cradled the flowers against her cheek. "One of my favorites starts out, 'Because I could not stop for Death— / He kindly stopped for me— / The Carriage held but just Ourselves— / And Immortality.' "

Morgan felt a chill as he saw the image of black-robed Death pulling up for him in a horse-drawn carriage. "Emily was kind of depressing, don't you think?"

Anne looked thoughtful, and he was struck again by the fathomless sadness in her eyes. "She was very original, and her imagery is wonderful."

"You sound like a teacher."

Anne laughed. "Sorry. I've always wished I could write poetry, so sometimes I get overly enthusiastic."

Morgan saw pollen left by the flowers on her cheek. He reached down and smoothed his thumb across her silky skin, then wished he'd kept his hands to himself. Touching her made him want to touch her more. "Whatever happened to old Emily?" he asked.

"She died a recluse. It must be sad to die alone. Yet, I don't think she was afraid of death. In another poem, she wrote, 'I never spoke with God, / Nor visited in heaven; / Yet certain am I of the spot / As if the checks were given.' "

"Is that why you come to the church? To contemplate poetry?"

Anne looked over her shoulder toward the simple white frame building. "No. I come to find peace."

Morgan thought her answer baffling, but on one level, he understood it perfectly. "If you find it, share it," he said. "I've always wondered what peace would feel like." Her eyebrows knitted together, but before she could ask him a question, he took her elbow and said, "Come on. We'd better start back before Maggie rings the dinner bell. On the way, we can talk about the picnic Skip's planned for next week. You are coming, aren't you?"

Anne sorted through her closet in vain. "It's no use," she grumbled to the empty room. She didn't have a single thing to wear on a picnic.

"What's the big deal?" Marti had asked that morning. "You throw on some jeans and a T-shirt."

The "big deal" for Anne was spending all afternoon and evening with Morgan. Ever since he'd caught her at the church, ever since he'd touched her cheek, listened to her talk about poetry, ridden home with her, and studied her so solemnly with his blue eyes, she'd been unable to think of anything else.

She'd never known anyone like him. All the boys back home in her school were like children compared with Morgan. He was guarded and mysterious. She yearned to know what motivated him, what made him so secretive and distant. "Forget it," she told herself. "Just have fun with him." She attacked her closet again.

Anne was still trying on outfits when Marti arrived. "Aren't you ready yet?" Marti wailed.

"Almost. Which looks better—the blue shirt or the red one?"

"The blue. Now, let's go. The guys are waiting down by the corral, and we need to get saddled up."

Hurriedly, Anne changed shirts and tugged on her boots. At the corral, she slipped Golden Star a lump of sugar and tossed a saddle over the horse's back. She tightened the cinch and swung her leg over. "What's keeping you?" she asked Marti.

"I'm all thumbs with this saddle," she complained. "How do you do it so quickly?"

Anne didn't tell her that her speed came from wanting to be with Morgan. "Lots of practice."

They rode through the yard to the edge of the fenced property near the barn and corral. Blond-haired, blue-eyed Skip couldn't take his eyes off Marti as they rode up. Anne noticed that Morgan smiled at her, but there was no gleam of adoration in his eyes like the one in Skip's.

They fell into a slow pace, with Skip and Marti riding in the lead. The sun beat down on Anne's back, and the air smelled like newly mown hay. "I thought you might be riding the bay by now," Anne remarked, noticing that Morgan was astride his regular quarter horse. "I've seen you working with him, and he looks tame to me."

"I ride him, but my uncle's giving me grief. He says that the horse spooks too easily and that he'll never make a work horse."

"Isn't it all right to have the horse just because he's beautiful? Just because you like him?"

"A horse has to earn its feed. That's my uncle's philosophy. As for me—I agree with you. I'd like to get the bay to the point where he's show-worthy."

"Have you done that kind of thing before?"

"I ride the rodeo circuit in the late summer, before we have to bring the cattle into the winter grazing range. When rodeos hit the small towns around here, people turn out for the fun. I'd like to exhibit the bay, ride in the parades."

"You really ride in rodeos?"

Morgan grinned. "Bronc busting's my favorite event."

"You actually ride a horse that wants to throw you?" She remembered the time she saw him tossed around the corral by the bay. He'd hit the ground with such a thud, she'd actually ached herself.

"It's good money."

"Aren't you afraid of getting hurt?"

"It goes with the sport. You know, 'no pain, no gain.'"

"The parade part seems more my speed. Waving at people from the back of a beautiful horse—yes, that's more like it."

"You need fancy gear for that—expensive saddles, clothing—lots of flash. Tourists like to see movie-star cowboys. The real thing isn't very glamorous."

She thought the real thing was very glamorous. "I've never been to a rodeo. It sounds like fun."

"Platte City has its Pioneer Days celebration soon. As part of it, there's a rodeo. I'll be riding in it."

"Pioneer Days? Can I come?"

"Sure. The whole ranch attends. You'll have a good time." He looked sideways at her. "After I ride, we could do something together—if you want to, that is."

If I want to! Anne could hardly keep from shouting. "I'd like that," she said calmly.

Morgan clucked, and his horse quickened his pace. "Come on. Let's catch up to Skip and Marti. If we're not careful, Skip will eat all the food before we get a bite."

Anne urged Golden Star to keep up, all the while smiling to herself. She was with daredevil Morgan on a golden Colorado afternoon. He'd invited her to a rodeo. She wished she could bottle the afternoon. Life was beautiful. If only she could make it last.

Nine

THEY RODE ACROSS grassy fields, up rocky terrain, through narrow rocky inclines. The ground flattened out again, and they crossed through a creek that gurgled over sparkling stones. The sun was setting when they came to a lone tree in the middle of a flower-studded field.

"We're here," Skip announced, reining in and dismounting.

"Where's 'here'?" Marti asked.

"Heaven," Morgan replied, swinging down from his horse.

Anne swung off Golden Star and glanced in every direction. She wanted to race across the field. She wanted to embrace the sky. "You're right—this place is heaven," she told him.

They removed the saddles from the horses and allowed the animals to graze. Skip spread out a blanket, and they opened a picnic basket. "How long did you plan to stay, Skip—until the next Ice Age? There's so much to eat!" Anne exclaimed.

He plopped down on the blanket, across from Morgan, who'd already staked his claim. "I wasn't sure what everybody'd want to eat. I brought fried chicken, tortillas, burritos—do you like these things?" he asked.

Marti made a face. "Never touch the stuff. I prefer lobster."

Skip looked crestfallen, and Marti laughed playfully. "Everything looks delicious."

Anne placed the tip of a chili pepper on her tongue. Immediately, her mouth felt on fire and her eyes began to water. "No fair! They're too hot!"

"Everything Spanish is hot," Marti said with a flirtatious, sidelong glance toward Skip.

He flopped backward dramatically. "I'm in love."

By the time they'd finished eating, the sun nestled between two mountain peaks. Morgan pulled Anne to her feet. "Let's take a walk."

They crossed the field, walking toward the setting sun. "Do you suppose poets could write about this view?" Morgan asked, pointing to the hues of pink and lavender in the sky.

"The world is so beautiful sometimes that I can hardly stand it." Anne kept thinking about the generous, anonymous benefactor who had given her the means to be in Colorado. How she longed to thank JWC. How she wished she could meet and know this person. Anne bent and gathered a handful of colored blossoms.

"You really like flowers, don't you?"

"I always have. My father told me that he first fell in love with my mother because she reminded him of an English garden." Anne laughed. "When I was little and hated taking baths, he'd say, 'Anne, one can always distinguish a great lady—the air around her smells like flowers.' "

"Did it get you in the tub?"

"Every time." She smiled at him.

"Marti told me that your mother died when you were young."

"That's true. I miss her still."

"Do you remember much about her?"

"It's difficult to remember. I know from her photographs that she was beautiful. Mostly, I recall small things."

"Such as?"

"She laughed a lot. I remember how she and Daddy would sit on the front steps and laugh together. Mother was British. Daddy met her while he was studying at Oxford. And she truly did smell like flowers." Anne closed her eyes and inhaled, as if the Colorado air might somehow import that other fragrance from across time.

She opened her eyes to see Morgan staring at her. She wondered what it would feel like to rest her head against his chest, the way she'd seen her mother do with her father. "What about your mother?" she asked, hoping her feelings weren't written on her face. "Was she descended from the Cheyenne grandmother?"

Morgan had avoided discussing his family, but now he felt secure and talked. "The Cheyenne is on my father's side. My mother was a beautiful woman too, but different from the way you described yours. Mama loved a good time. She should never have gotten married. And she and my dad should *never* have had a kid."

Anne felt sorry for Morgan, for the hurt look that surfaced on his face. Had his mother treated him badly? "What about your father?" She expected Morgan to say that his mother had run away with another man and that his father was around somewhere.

"My dad's dead."

The matter-of-fact way he said it shocked Anne. "I see," she said, without seeing at all. Did that mean that his mother had abandoned Morgan—simply walked out of his life? And how had his father died? Morgan didn't add anything, although Anne gave him plenty of time. "How long have you been living with your aunt and uncle?" she asked after an awkward silence.

"Six years."

"Your aunt cares about you. I can tell."

"I know," Morgan said. "She's my dad's sister. We have a lot in common." Talking about his parents had depressed him. Recalling the look of love in Anne's eyes when she spoke about her parents only intensified his pain. He pitied the little girl whose mother had died and left her behind. He ached for the twelve-year-old boy he'd been when his father had been taken away and his mother had packed her things and left, even though he understood—still understood—why she had. He honestly didn't hold it against her.

His mother's words came back clearly, although it

had been almost seven years. *"I can't stay. I can't sit around year after year and wait for this to happen to either Maggie or you. No one should have to have this happen. No one. It's a living nightmare."*

"Has our conversation depressed you?" Anne's question pulled Morgan back into the present.

"No way," he replied, forcing a smile. Looking over her shoulder, he could see Skip and Marti kissing. He wanted to kiss Anne too. He wanted to take her in his arms and kiss her until the fear inside him went away. "I learned to live with it a long time ago."

Anne didn't want to challenge him, but she was certain he'd never learned to live with what had happened to him. She gazed skyward and saw that stars were beginning to appear. "I've never seen so many stars," she said, hoping to recapture their earlier mood. "In New York City, you have to go to an observatory to see this kind of star power."

Morgan looked up and studied the star-studded night. "Out here, you take some things for granted. Night skies full of stars is only one of them." Pretty, rich girls from big cities, whom he didn't want to become involved with, were another.

"Look!" Anne cried, pointing heavenward. "A shooting star!"

Morgan watched the star streak across the night. "Some nights, it seems like the whole universe is falling to earth."

Anne could only imagine. Still staring upward, she heard Morgan say, "We should head back. It's a long ride home." She followed him back to the blanket, disappointed. Marti was making repairs to her lipstick, and Skip looked thoroughly kissed. For a moment, Anne felt a sharp twinge of envy. If only Morgan felt that way about her.

"We need to saddle up," Morgan told Skip.

"So soon? Marti has the whole night off."

"Well, I don't," Morgan said, forcing Anne to believe that he was making up an excuse to be rid of her.

Skip touched Morgan's shoulder and whispered, "Is it because of what her old man said?"

Anne heard his words and whipped around in time to catch the warning glare Morgan shot to Skip. Skip shuffled self-consciously and began folding the blanket. Flabbergasted, she stood rooted to the ground. She felt shock, then humiliation. Had her father *dared* to go to Morgan behind her back? Had he actually said something to him about her condition?

Her fingers were stiff as she saddled her horse, but once they were all on the trail, she couldn't keep silent. Skip and Marti were lagging behind them this time, and once Anne was sure they were out of earshot, she said, "I heard what Skip said back there."

"I figured you did. He's got the tact of a skunk."

"Don't be mad at him. I'm glad I overheard. What did my dad say to you?"

"It's not important."

"It is to me." Her heart was pounding, and her hands trembled on the reins.

"He didn't threaten me or anything. I know he's only concerned about you."

In the dark, she couldn't make out his expression. "He didn't threaten you?"

"He asked me to leave you alone, that's all."

Her anger flared, but she bit it back. "I wasn't aware you were bothering me."

"All right. . . . he doesn't want us spending so much time together. He doesn't want me to get too involved."

"Why?"

"It's a fact of life, Anne—fathers who bring their daughters out to the Broken Arrow for a summer vacation don't want them to get sidetracked by some dumb cowboy who's got nothing to show for his life. I'm not well educated. I'm not wealthy. I'm not any of the things fathers want for their daughters. I understand his feelings."

"Well, I don't! He had no right—"

"He had every right."

"My dad and I don't have that kind of relationship." How could she explain it to Morgan, who had no father and who argued with his uncle about control of his life? "My father's always given me space to make my own choices. He's never imposed his will on mine. And he's always trusted me. It's just now that . . ."

"Let's just forget it," Morgan said. He clucked to his horse, urging it to a canter.

Anne balled the reins in her fist in total frustration. She broke out in a cold, clammy sweat. She dug her heels into Golden Star's side and rode in a slow gallop all the way back to the ranch.

Ten

"DIDN'T WE HAVE a ball?" Marti asked.

"Sure. A great time was had by all."

"Maybe you were right about my giving other guys a chance. Maybe I deserve to see what there is beside Peter. Maybe we can do this again soon."

"Maybe so. I'll catch you tomorrow."

"Sure . . ." Marti's voice trailed off as Anne hurried toward her cabin. She didn't want to be rude to Marti, but she had plenty to tell her father.

Her father was sitting outside on the steps when she arrived. "Did you have fun?" he asked.

Anne felt betrayed and didn't bother to hide it. "Waiting up for me? You haven't done that since I was thirteen."

"Whoa . . . wait a minute. I'm just breathing in all this wonderful fresh air you're always telling me about. What's the problem? You sound as if you're indicting me."

She crossed her arms and stood in front of him. "I know that you told Morgan to leave me alone."

"How do you know that?"

"It came out in conversation."

"It simply 'came out'? Did he tell you?"

Anne recognized her father's attempt to put her on the defensive. She figured it was a skill teachers must cultivate in order to deal with belligerent students. "Why did you do it, Dad? Why would you tell him such a thing when you know I want a normal life."

He sighed heavily and urged her to sit beside him on the steps. "All right, maybe I did question him about his motives toward you."

"His motives? What are you—a detective?"

"You're infatuated with him, Anne."

She felt her cheeks color. Were her feelings so obvious that her father could read them from a distance? "I've never known anyone like Morgan before."

"Anne, this type of attraction is a first for you. It's been a long time coming, but the time has arrived. I've never seen you interested in a boy before, and it's . . . difficult for me."

She hated the way he made her special feelings for Morgan sound so common and ordinary, as if they made up some kind of phase *everybody* went through. "You must think I'm a real social reject."

"I think you're beautiful, talented, smart, and heads and hands above any of the overly hormone-infused teenage boys from high school. I knew none of them could ever hold your interest."

"You're my father—of course, you think I'm one of a kind."

"As your father," he said, "I've been both anticipating and dreading this day for years. The day when you'd meet a guy who saw you for the wonderful person you are. And wanted you in every way."

She was missing her mother again. "You make it sound like I'm some raw, throbbing hormone, waiting to be pounced upon by some guy." In spite of her irritation, Anne smiled. "You can't be worried that I might trip and fall into his bed. We both know why."

When her father answered, she knew he'd given his reply much thought. "Sometimes, when I look at you, I still see that gangly eleven-year-old with the bruised knees and scraped elbows. It's difficult accepting that you're a grown woman. That you're feeling all the emotions of a normal sixteen-year-old. I never wanted to think of you growing up and getting involved with any man . . . not even the one you marry and now . . ."

"Except we both know that I'll never marry, don't we?"

She saw that his eyes were damp. "Sometimes, when I think about what's happening to you, it's more than I can bare. Sometimes, I wake in the middle of the night, and I'm sweating and shaking, and I can't catch my breath. I can't believe all that's being taken away from you. It isn't right. It isn't fair.

I'd give anything to have the disease and see you free of it. But I can't."

First, he lost her mother; now, he was losing her. Not in a normal way of giving her away in marriage. But to premature death. Just for the moment, she caught the impact of his anguish. "Daddy, I've been trying to sort out answers for myself about what's happened to me. I've thought about little else. Not just 'why me?' but why people have to suffer in the first place. Maybe we're not supposed to understand. Maybe all we can do is accept what we can't change, and keep on going. I realized that after mom died or I couldn't have gone on."

"It sounds as if you've examined life's imponderables with far more maturity than I have given you credit for," her father commented.

"That's what I've been doing when I haven't been riding, or looking longingly at Morgan."

He gave a quiet, sad laugh. "I don't feel I'm doing enough to help you. Enough to protect you."

"I'll need you most when we go home. When I get really sick."

"I'll be there for you. I'll never desert you, Anne." He pulled her to his side and kissed the top of her head. "In the meantime, you be careful around Morgan. Don't do anything foolish. I don't want you to have a broken heart too. I can't fix that either."

Anne wondered how she could be anything but careful. She knew what was at stake. Perhaps her father was right. Perhaps it would be best to stay away from Morgan altogether. To completely shield him from harm's way. After all, if he ever knew she was exposing him to HIV, what would he do?

Perhaps it had been a mistake to come to the Broken Arrow. She thought about JWC and for the hundredth time wondered what had possessed a person she didn't know to give her so much money. Surely, JWC and the One Last Wish Foundation had made a mistake. In receiving the money before the onset of actual AIDS, Anne had squandered some of it foolishly and chosen a path that was leading to heartache.

And yet, she was glad she'd met Morgan, who had the power to make her heart skip a beat with a mere glance. If it hadn't been for the Wish money, she would have never met him. And if she'd been perfectly healthy, their relationship still would have come to nothing more than a summer fling, she reminded herself. After all, what could he possibly find exciting about a inexperienced girl who knew nothing about love, who picked wildflowers and loved poetry?

It didn't take a genius to figure it out. Anne was avoiding him. "Chalk one up for Daddy," Morgan told himself sourly as he pitched hay in the barn one afternoon. Why was he surprised? Snobby little rich girls were all alike.

He should have just gone ahead and had a good time with her physically when he'd had the opportunity. But, no . . . he'd backed off, kept his hands to himself, all because—

His thoughts were interrupted when he heard someone come into the barn. He looked over the edge of the loft and saw Anne wandering aimlessly around the quiet barn. She was hugging a book and looking for a place to sit. *Why does she have to come in here?* He didn't need the aggravation.

He watched her settle on a mound of hay and open her book. He wished he'd taken to books—maybe then the two of them would have more in common. He decided that he wasn't going to hide from her, ignore her the way she'd been ignoring him. Morgan began to whistle, tossed a forkful of hay down from the loft, and saw it land near Anne's feet.

A startled cry escaped from her, which gave Morgan some satisfaction. He shimmied down from the loft. "Sorry," he said. "I thought I was alone in here."

"Me too." Anne started to rise, but when she planted her hand in the hay to give herself a boost, she yelped in pain.

"What's wrong?" Morgan started toward her. She lifted her hand, and he saw a line of bright red blood across her palm. He felt a sickening sensation in his stomach. "There must be something sharp under the hay. Don't move." He knelt beside her.

Fearfully, she stared at her bleeding hand.

Morgan reached beneath her, lifted her, and placed her safely away from the hay and its invisible weapon. "Let me see how bad you're cut."

"It's nothing," Anne said, keeping her hand close to her body. "I'm fine."

"You're not fine. You're bleeding. You may need stitches. Let me wipe it off and examine it."

Her eyes widened, reminding him of a deer trapped in headlights. "No! Don't touch it!"

"Why? I want to help. I've seen blood before."

"Stay away! Please, don't touch me." She was shaking all over.

"At least let me wrap my handkerchief around it to try to stop the bleeding." He fumbled in his jeans pocket.

"No!" She darted backward. "My father and I'll take care of it."

"But—"

"Please—you don't understand. I-I can't explain. Just don't touch it." Wild-eyed, panicked, she spun, and clutching her hand to her side, she bolted from the barn.

Dumbfounded, Morgan watched her run back toward her cabin.

Eleven

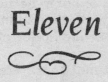

"LET ME SEE your hand. Does it hurt?" Marti looked worried at the dinner table that night.

"It's nothing," Anne insisted. "The doctor in Platte City put a bandage on it and gave me a tetanus shot. Talk about something that hurt—" She rubbed her arm, hoping to distract Marti.

"Morgan acted impossible all afternoon. He felt it was his fault."

"He had nothing to do with it. I cut my hand, that's all." Her eyes met her father's over Marti's head. When it had happened, all she could think about was Morgan's touching her blood and somehow absorbing the HIV into himself. And when she had to face the doctor in Platte City, when she had to tell him to take extra precautions before treating her, the reality of her situation almost devastated her. "We should leave," she'd told her father in the car coming back to the ranch. "We should go home before I infect somebody."

"Nonsense," her father had said. "If we leave, it'll be because you truly want to go. You're not a threat to anybody. Do you want to leave?"

Anne felt she was a threat. She also felt dishonest because she wasn't telling people the truth about herself. Did her friends have a right to know? A right to choose whether or not to be around her? She felt like a coward because she couldn't bring herself to tell them. Or to see the horror on their faces once they knew.

"*Oya!* Listen to me, Anne," Marti was saying. "I want to know if we can go into Platte City for Pioneer Days on Friday. I have the whole day off, and I want to go have some fun."

"I thought you were going with Skip."

Marti glanced around, then leaned closer. "He'll meet me in the afternoon, after the rodeo. You and I can see the sights until Skip's free."

"I don't know . . ." She remembered when Morgan had suggested she come to the celebration with him. After the way she'd been acting, he would probably be keeping his distance from her.

"You can't tell me no," Marti said, with a quick smile.

Anne shook her finger at Marti, who giggled and called over her shoulder, "The van for Platte City leaves from the main lodge Friday morning, and you'd better be in it with me."

On Friday, a whole crowd of guests rode into the small city. A large banner hung over the main street, proclaiming Pioneer Days, and booths and stands selling food, arts and crafts items, and western memorabilia lined the thoroughfare. People jostled along the sidewalk, and set up chairs down the side of the street for the parade scheduled at high noon.

"Isn't this fun?" Marti asked. She and Anne strolled down the sidewalk, licking ice-cream cones.

"*Si,*" Anne replied in Spanish. "*Estoy muy—*" she struggled to remember the Spanish word for 'fun' and ended up saying, "—fun!"

Marti laughed gaily. "What an accent! Come on, let's grab a spot to watch the parade."

They sat on a curb, and when the parade started, Anne discovered they were in a perfect position to see everything. Marching bands, convertibles filled with pretty girls, clowns, and riders astride different breeds of horses passed directly in front of them. Anne identified groups of palominos, pintos, paso finos, quarter horses, and purebred Arabians, ridden by men, women, even children dressed in western and Mexican clothing.

"Look, there's Skip," Marti said. She waved to a clown dressed in baggy pants, an oversized shirt, and a flaming red wig. His face was painted white, except for exaggerated drawn-on red lips.

"How can you tell?" Anne teased. Skip stepped from the parade line and handed them both balloons. "You look adorable," Anne told him.

"Thanks. Are you both coming to the rodeo? I'll be working the ring, and Morgan's going to ride," he said.

"Clowns work in rodeos?" Anne asked.

"Important work. We distract the wild bulls when a rider gets thrown."

"How? Do the bulls fall down laughing?" Anne kidded, but the image of Morgan's being thrown from the back of a bucking horse flashed through her mind.

"Very funny," Skip said as Marti giggled.

"Don't you ride the broncos or bulls?" Anne asked.

"Do I look crazy? Not this boy. I participate in the roping events and the barrel races." He glanced at the passing parade. "I'd better catch up." He grabbed Marti's hand. "March with me."

"I can't."

"Sure you can. You and Anne can hook up in the stands at the rodeo."

Anne could see that Marti wanted to go with Skip. She gave her a nudge. "Go on. I'll shop and meet you in an hour."

Once Marti and Skip had joined the parade, Anne settled back onto the curb. A group of riders was coming down the street with a banner heralding the Broken Arrow. As they passed, she recognized many of the ranch's workers. Her breath caught when she saw Morgan riding the prancing bay range horse. He'd tamed him! Her heart swelled proudly, and she waved, but she wasn't sure Morgan saw her.

When the parade ended and the crowd broke up, Anne wandered through a few stores, buying souvenirs for friends back home. In so many ways, she felt like a normal tourist with nothing to do but have a good time. If only it were true. "No negative thoughts," she told herself sternly.

She entered a western-wear shop and browsed, admiring fringed, buttery-soft buckskin jackets, a pair of snakeskin boots, and elaborate western shirts, encrusted with appliqués, sequins, and glittering jewels. On one wall, she saw ornate Stetson hats, chaps, and leather belts. But it was a saddle sitting atop a sawhorse that took away her breath.

The saddle was black leather, decorated with sterling silver. Anne fingered the saddle's rich, hand-carved depressions and ran her palm over the intricate silver design patterns. She'd never seen anything like it, never knew such a utilitarian piece of equipment could be made to look so beautiful.

In her mind's eye, she saw it across the back of Morgan's bay stallion. She remembered what Morgan had told her about wanting to show his horse and how expensive proper show gear was to buy. She lifted the price tag and raised her eyebrows. The saddle cost almost two thousand dollars. She chewed her bottom lip. How she'd like to buy it for him!

Her mind returned to the time in the hospital when she'd discovered the OLW envelope on her pillow, and to the sense of absolute awe she'd experienced when she'd seen the check, the enormous amount of money given to her by someone she didn't even know. Hadn't the letter said, ". . . *the true miracle is in giving, not receiving*"?

While Anne knew she couldn't keep the origin of such a gift as the saddle from Morgan, she certainly had money enough to buy it for him. Moreover, she *wanted* to buy it for him, wanted him to feel what she'd felt when JWC had unexpectedly blessed her life. Heart pounding, Anne made up her mind and found a clerk.

After she'd acquired the saddle, a matching bridle, and a handwoven saddle blanket, she made arrangements for her purchases to be delivered to the Broken Arrow the following day. Pleased with herself, she followed the crowds to the outdoor rodeo arena, where she found Marti already perched in the stands for the show.

"I thought you'd gotten lost," Marti said.

"Just sidetracked. Did you have a good time?"

"The best time. I like Skip so much. He's sweet and kind and treats me like I'm special."

"You are special," Anne said.

Marti dropped her gaze. "It makes me realize how badly Peter has treated me, and I've taken it like a fool."

Once the rodeo began, Anne lost herself completely in the atmosphere. The barrel race had several age categories, three won by cowgirls. Skip placed second in the men's group, and Marti cheered more loudly than anyone in the stands for him.

The sun was setting and the arena was lit by overhead stadium lights when it came time for the bronco-riding events. Anne felt jittery. The object was for the rider to stay on the horse for as long as possible. A buzzer would sound at the end of a specific time period, and any rider who was still mounted became a finalist. "What's the prize?" Anne asked.

"A hundred dollars," Marti told her.

Anne didn't think it sounded like enough money for such a brain-rattling, teeth-jarring event, but she kept quiet. The first rider out of the chute was tossed off like a rag doll. Anne winced as he thudded onto the ground. Yet, he got up, dusted himself off, and hurried out of the ring while other riders captured the bucking horse and led it back to the holding pen.

By the time she heard Morgan's name called, her jaw hurt from clenching her teeth. She watched as he swung from the side of the special chute onto the back of a horse called Loco. "A horse named Crazy," Marti remarked. "He must be some mean one."

Anne saw Morgan wrap a gloved hand around a rope tied to the horse and raise the other hand into the air above his head in the classic one-handed posture of bronco riders. A bell rang, the gate opened, and Loco exploded into the arena.

The horse gyrated and twisted itself into impossible contortions. He hit the ground stiff-legged, his head pulled low, his eyes white with wild fury. Morgan twisted with him, gripping the horse's heaving sides with his knees. To Anne, it seemed an eternity until the buzzer sounded. The audience erupted into cheers.

Morgan released his hold on the rope and kicked himself off the animal's back. As he dropped, his boot caught in the rope. Suddenly, he was hanging sideways from the horse, unable to get off. Morgan dangled helplessly from the furious animal as it continued its mad twisting and bucking, its deadly hooves lifting off the ground, inches from Morgan's head.

A cry raced through the crowd as the spectators grasped his deadly predicament. Anne froze, watching in horror. All at once, the arena filled with clowns and men on quarter horses chasing after the bronco. One clown waved a blanket, causing the horse to stop abruptly. Quickly, two mounted cowboys came alongside Loco, sandwiched the wild horse between them and snatched his headgear, forcing him to stand still.

Clowns helped loosen Morgan's trapped foot and lower him to the ground. Others baring a stretcher ran into the arena and lifted him on it. Through her daze, Anne heard Marti yell, "They're taking him to the hospital tent!"

Twelve

ANNE RACED OUT and turned down a path, made narrow by parked horse trailers. At the far end, she saw a large tent with a red cross painted on its side, and rushed toward it. Outside, a woman wearing an armband bearing the same red cross stopped her. "Can I help you?" she asked.

Flustered, Anne groped for words. "They brought in a rider from the arena ... he'd been thrown, dragged. I need to see how he is. He's a friend."

The nurse offered a reassuring smile. "Calm down. The doctor's taping him up now. He's got a couple of cracked ribs, some bruises and contusions, but he's going to be fine."

Anne felt her knees buckle with relief. "He won't have to go to the hospital?"

"I think he refused to go."

"Do you suppose I could go in and see him?"

"You'll have to wait in line—his family's in with him now. They looked plenty scared—and hopping mad!"

"Are you positive he's all right?"

The nurse reached out, took her hand, and said, "Don't take it so hard, honey. These cowboys are a pretty tough bunch. I've seen men stomped on by bulls weighing a ton, and they still get up to ride another day."

The tent flap opened, and a man in a lab coat stepped outside. "The boy doing okay?" the nurse asked.

"Miraculously, yes. The X rays showed no breaks other than his ribs, but that ride wrenched several muscles. He's going to be sore for a while."

"See, I told you not to worry," the nurse said to Anne.

Anne still wanted to see Morgan. "Go on, honey. Go see for yourself," the nurse said.

Smiling gratefully, Anne entered the tent carefully. Morgan was shirtless, sitting up on an examining table, a thick swath of adhesive bandage wound around his torso. Standing directly in front of him were his aunt and uncle.

She heard his uncle's angry voice, ". . . can't believe the chance you took!"

"I've ridden in plenty of rodeos. I just had some back luck today."

"Bad luck! You almost got killed!"

"I *like* to ride," Morgan replied stubbornly.

"No one cares if you ride in rodeo events," Aunt Maggie interjected. "But what's wrong with the barrel races? Or the calf roping?"

Morgan snorted. "They're not my style."

"Almost getting yourself killed is more your style?" Uncle Don shook his finger in Morgan's face. "You know what your problem is? You've got a death wish, boy! You won't be happy until you *die* out there."

"Stop it," Aunt Maggie commanded, grabbing her husband's arm. "Carrying on here and now isn't helping anything." She stepped closer to Morgan and took his face between her hands. "Oh, Morgan, you scared us to death."

Morgan looked into her eyes. "Sorry, Aunt Maggie," he mumbled.

"You're all the family I have left, Morgan. I don't want to lose you. Please, please stop this crazy, reckless way of living. Why do you do it?"

Anne saw Morgan reach up and wipe a tear from his aunt's cheek. "You, of all people, understand *why*, Aunt Maggie. You know more than anyone what might lie ahead for either one—or both—of us. You and me . . . we're different from the others."

"That may be true, but I'm living with it without risking my life. Somehow, you've got to make your peace about it."

"I can't."

Anne felt like an eavesdropper. What in the world were they talking about? What was "different" about Morgan and his aunt? They looked normal. *So do you*, she reminded herself. Could anyone tell by simply *looking* at another person what lay in the darkness of his or her life?

Uncle Don cleared his throat. "I didn't mean to be so hard on you," he said gruffly. "Maggie and I are really glad they could patch you up." He put his arm around his wife's shoulders. "We'll load your horse up in the trailer and take him back to the ranch for you."

"Thanks."

"Come with us," Aunt Maggie said.

"I'll catch a ride with Skip. I'm fine. Stop worrying about me."

His aunt and uncle both hugged him, turned, and walked toward the tent's exit. Passing Anne, they gave her a brief nod of recognition. She felt out of place. Morgan saw her. "Why are you here?" he asked, registering surprise.

"I saw you get thrown. I was concerned." She came toward him.

He edged off the table, wincing with the movement. "No need to be. Besides, I look pretty awful—and I know how the sight of blood gets to you."

"Only my own," she said humorlessly.

He picked up his torn shirt and attempted to put it on.

"Let me help," Anne offered, taking it from him and easing it along his arms. She stepped in front of him and began to button it. His face was inches from hers, and he was looking down at hers. Her breath caught, and her heart began to hammer crazily. "All finished," she said, slightly breathless.

He caught both her hands with one of his and settled them at the base of his throat. She felt the warmth of his pulse. "Are you?" he asked.

Torn with a desire she could barely suppress, Anne gently tugged her hands loose and stepped backward. "We should be going."

Morgan eyed her patiently, then reached for his hat. "I should have accepted a ride home with Uncle Don," he admitted. "I really am pretty sore."

Anne felt the air still humming between them. "Maybe Skip's ready to go on back by now."

"Let's go find out."

They rode to the ranch in Skip's old pickup truck with Marti fussing over Morgan, half scolding him in Spanish, half rejoicing that he hadn't been killed. Anne rode in silence, cramped for space, trying not to lean against Morgan's taped ribs. In the darkness, her hands trembled. She was unable to forget how much she'd wanted to put her arms around him.

At the men's quarters, Skip helped Morgan from the truck. "I'll drive the girls around," Skip said.

"Drive Marti," Morgan told him, taking hold of Anne's hand. "Let Anne stay with me for a while."

"I shouldn't," Anne said, knowing she should climb up into the truck and get out of there quickly.

"I'll need some help," Morgan countered.

The row of housing looked empty and deserted, and Anne realized that everyone was probably still in Platte City. She gulped and, against her better judgment, agreed to help him to his room.

Morgan's room was small, sparsely furnished, but tidy. It contained a table and two chairs, a bureau, a single bed, a TV, and a stereo system. A small refrigerator, a microwave, and a sink for washing dishes lined one wall. She wondered why he chose to live alone with the hired hands rather than in the comfort of the main lodge with his aunt and uncle. She knew without question that they would have allowed him such a privilege.

"I like living here," he explained, as if reading her mind.

Anne's hands fluttered nervously. "You've done a nice job with the room."

"Probably not anything like what you're used to."

Puzzled, she didn't know how to answer. "Maybe I should get you settled before Skip comes back for me."

"He'll be a while."

"He does seem to like Marti, doesn't he? I think they make a cute couple. Don't you?" Anne felt as if she were babbling.

Morgan eased onto his bed, propping the pillow against the headboard, and snapped on the bedside lamp. "Turn off the overhead, will you? It's hurting my eyes." She flipped off the main light switch with shaking fingers. "Come here," he said.

She came, and he urged her to sit on the side of the bed. She felt like a moth drawn to a flame. "Don't your ribs hurt?" she asked.

"Like crazy." He reached up and ran his fingers through her long, dark hair.

She quivered. He turned off the lamp, and suddenly moonlight streamed through the window over his bed. Squares of white light stretched across the spread and dripped onto the floor. By now, Anne's heart was thudding so fast that she was certain her body couldn't contain it. Her bones felt like warm liquid.

He pulled her closer and kissed her forehead, her temple, her closed eyelids. "Stay with me, Anne," she heard Morgan whisper. "Please stay the night."

Thirteen

STAY WITH ME. Anne heard the words echoing in her brain, felt the yearning they carved inside her heart. To stay with Morgan, to spend a night in his arms, to taste a world she'd only read about in books and poetry. . . . "Skip will be coming back for me soon," she said.

"Skip will pull up outside and honk. If you don't go out, he'll drive away." Morgan cupped her chin and stroked her hair. "You must know how much I want to be with you, Anne. I've tried to stay away from you, tried to pretend that I wasn't attracted to you, but for the life of me, I can't pretend anymore. You're very beautiful, and I want you very much."

For the life of me. The words fell like hammer blows into a core of cool logic inside her mind. What he was asking of her could cost him his life. She'd read about, heard about, and knew how to practice safe sex, but in one heartrending moment, she realized that such safety could be illusionary. And one chance, even one in a million, was one too many for her to risk his life, no matter how much she wanted to stay with him. "I can't stay." Dragging out the words was difficult.

"Why?"

"I just can't." She pulled away from his arms and stood, struggling to keep her voice steady.

"Anne—"

"I think I should wait outside for Skip. I think you should get some rest." She was trembling all over.

He looked up at her, and in the swath of moonlight, he looked wounded. "Sure. Whatever you want."

Anne felt tears jamming up behind her eyes. She fumbled for the doorknob. It felt cold and hard in her grip. Once she stepped out of the room, this part of her life would dissipate like smoke. She wanted to run back to him, throw herself in his arms, and beg him to hold her, kiss her. She knew in that moment that she loved him, but could never tell him.

"Good-bye," she whispered. And with more bravery than she ever dreamed she possessed, Anne stepped quickly into the night.

She arose early the next morning and went straight to the lodge. The aroma of fresh coffee, sizzling bacon, and baking biscuits filled the air, and a radio played country music in the background.

When she entered, Morgan struggled up from one

of the sofas and came toward her. "Morning," he said. His eyes looked guarded.

"You feeling all right?" she asked, her heart thudding.

"I ache all over. Uncle Don's relieved me of my duties for the next week; the doctor told us it'll take at least six weeks for the ribs to completely heal. Anyway, I'm supposed to be taking it easy."

"Then you should still be in bed, resting."

"I wanted to talk to you. I wanted to apologize for last night."

Anne nervously glanced down at the floor. "There's nothing to apologize for."

"I was out of line. I never should have asked you what I did."

She didn't want him taking it back. She wanted to think, even now, that he'd meant what he'd said. "It's okay. Forget it."

"I guess that bronco rattled my brain," Morgan said with a sincere smile. "I'm sorry if I insulted you."

"You didn't insult me."

"Then you're not angry at me?"

"I'm not."

Morgan tipped the brim of his hat to her, then limped painfully away.

Anne thought the matter was settled and that she and Morgan were finished, so when Maggie asked her to go see Morgan down in the barn, she was surprised and mystified. She hurried to the barn, eager to spend any time she could near him. When she came in out of the hot, bright sun, she saw Morgan leaning against the gate of a stall, the fancy leather-and-silver saddle thrown over it.

"It came!" Anne cried, hurrying over. She'd forgotten all about it. "Do you like it?"

"I thought my apology was enough." His voice sounded cool.

Anne felt her smile fade. "I don't know what you mean."

"Did you think you had to soothe my feelings with this?"

She was confused by his hostility. "I thought you'd like it. That you would use it on the bay, during parades. I thought you'd be pleased."

He shook his head and pushed stiffly away from the stall. "You little rich girls are all alike. You think that you can buy anybody's favor, purchase anything you want with Daddy's money."

"Rich?" She couldn't believe his assumption. "What makes you think I'm rich?"

"I know what that saddle cost. I've looked at it many times. Don't tell me you didn't spend a fortune on it."

Anne was speechless. She wanted to tell him she wasn't wealthy, hadn't been born into the lap of luxury. Yet, how could she explain? She clamped her lips tightly. There was no way, of course. It was far better to allow Morgan to cling to his false assumptions about her than for her to explain reality. "It's a gift, Morgan, with no strings, no hidden motives."

"I don't want it."

She held her head high. "It's yours anyway. If you really don't want it, you can throw it in the garbage, for all I care. Rich girls like me can buy others." She spun, kicking up dust and hay with her boots, and jogged quickly away from the barn and the gleaming saddle.

The next week dragged for Anne. She didn't feel well, either. Her glands were swollen, and a persistent cough plagued her. Sometimes she awoke in the night sweating profusely. Her appetite decreased, but she attributed that to the unhappiness she felt over her estrangement from Morgan.

One afternoon, a steady rain forced all activity on the ranch to a standstill. Anne confined herself to a game of solitaire in the main lodge, hardly noticing the guests who grouped around the TV set and board games. From the corner of her eye, she saw Morgan sitting on the hearth of the great stone fireplace. He was entertaining a group of kids with a length of rope, showing them how to tie different kinds of knots.

A violent clap of thunder shook the rafters. Anne started, and kids squealed, scampering toward their mothers like frightened kittens. "It's only a big boomer," Anne heard Maggie explain to everyone. "My mama used to say thunder was only the angels bowling up in heaven."

Laughter rippled through the room. "Fall's coming," Maggie added. "Summer rain means autumn's on its way."

Anne didn't want to think about autumn, because it meant she'd be back home, and if her health held, she'd be back in school. She'd miss the outdoors, Golden Star, Maggie, Marti, Skip, Morgan—most of all, Morgan.

Suddenly, the door of the lodge banged and Skip

stood framed in the open doorway. His yellow slicker streamed with water that puddled on the floor around his boots. "Morgan!" Skip shouted. "You'd better come quick. Your bay bolted, tried to jump the fence. He's hurt. Bad."

Fourteen

MORGAN GOT UP too fast, and a stabbing pain shot through his side. He clamped his hand over his taped, bruised ribs and limped toward Skip. "What happened?" he asked.

"The thunder must have spooked him. I was in the barn and looked out in time to see him try to jump the corral fence. There wasn't enough room for a running start, of course, and he went crashing through the poles."

Morgan felt a sickening sensation in the pit of his stomach. "Is he up?"

"Last I saw, he was thrashing on the ground. I came to find you, quick as I could."

Morgan didn't wait for further explanations. He shoved past Skip and hurried outside into the driving rain faster than his aching side wanted him to move. If his horse was still down, it meant only one thing—he was too hurt to get up. Horses instinctively sought to stay upright.

The rain was driving so hard, Morgan could barely navigate his way to the corral. He was drenched to the skin and trying to maneuver through the mud. He arrived at the corral, but the rain was so heavy, he couldn't see from one side to the other. Skip caught up with him. "This way," Skip yelled.

Gasping for breath, Morgan hobbled after him; his lungs felt on fire. The horse was lying on the ground, one of its legs twisted at an angle. The animal continued to thrash, but its movements looked weak. Morgan crouched by the bay's head. Its eyes were wide with fright. "Take it easy, fella," Morgan said, stroking the animal's neck.

Skip knelt beside him. "It's bad, isn't it?" He had to shout to be heard above the rain.

"The worst. Uncle Don always said the horse was spooky. I should have listened to him, should never have tried to make him my own."

"Don't blame yourself."

The horse was one more thing he'd loved and lost. Morgan rose painfully and steeled himself for what he knew he had to do. The horse would have to be put down. The ranch couldn't afford to nurse a horse that had value only to him and that would probably never be right even if he did heal. Feed and veterinarians cost money. "Dumb, hardheaded beast," Morgan said to himself, trying to distance himself emotionally.

"You want me to take over?" Skip asked.

"I can handle it." Morgan felt a coldness inside himself, similar to the one he'd felt when he'd learned about his father.

"You sure?"

Morgan nodded.

Skip went into the barn and emerged with Morgan's rifle. He handed it to him.

"What are you doing?" Anne's frantic question above the roar of the rain took Morgan and Skip by surprise.

Morgan turned, ignoring the pain in his side from too quick a movement. "Get out of here," he said.

"I won't! What are you going to do?" Her eyes looked wide and frightened. The rain had plastered her clothing to her body, and her hair hung in soaked ringlets.

She tried to march past Morgan and Skip, but Morgan caught her around the waist and pushed her toward Skip. "Take her back to the lodge," he ordered.

Anne struggled. "I won't go! You're going to shoot him, aren't you? You're going to kill your horse!"

"His leg is broken, and he's suffering. It's the humane thing to do."

"But there are doctors—vets . . . you could call someone . . ."

"Get her out of here, Skip."

Skip tried to pull her gently away. "Come on, Anne."

She broke from Skip and hurled herself at Morgan. "How can you do such a thing? I don't understand how you can be so heartless."

Morgan raised the rifle, cocked the firing mechanism. "Don't you know, Anne? Life's cruel."

She drew herself up tall and glared straight into his icy blue eyes. "Not life," she said. "People are cruel."

Anne shook off Skip's hold on her elbow, spun, and ran as hard and fast as she could. She shivered. She was so wet and cold that her teeth chattered. She didn't care. Nothing mattered, nothing except putting distance between Morgan and his shattered horse, and herself.

From far away, she heard the sharp, distinctive crack of a rifle. Anne covered her ears and cried out as if the bullet had hit her.

Anne stayed in bed all the following day. Her body ached, and she felt a pressure in her chest, as if weights were pressing against her, making it difficult to breathe.

"I've called Dr. Rinaldi in Denver," her father fumed. "How could you allow yourself to get drenched yesterday? You know your immune system can't handle this."

Anne was too weak, too ill to argue. Her father bundled her up, put her in the backseat of the ranch's station wagon, and drove much too fast all the way into the city. After Dr. Rinaldi examined her, he wrote several prescriptions. "You've got pneumonia. For an HIV-positive person, this is extremely dangerous. You'll need to be hospitalized immediately."

She tried to protest.

"You can't put off going onto the AZT any longer.

I believe that your blood work will show that your
T4 cells have fallen drastically. Let me check you in
to the hospital, start you on AZT, and get your infection under control."

She shook her head. "I want to go home, back to
New York City." She looked to her father. "Can you
get us a plane to New York tomorrow?" Anne felt
surprisingly calm. "We can pack and be to the air-
port by morning," she said.

"I'll pack. You rest," her father said. "Doctor, can
she manage the trip?"

The doctor spoke against it, but finally admitted it
was their choice.

They arrived back at the ranch late, but Anne insisted on saying good-bye to Marti. They'd be leaving before dawn. Anne slipped into the cabin and
shook Marti's shoulder.

"Is it time to get up already? I feel like I just went
to bed." Marti rubbed her eyes. "Is that you, Anne?
What are you doing here? Is something wrong?"

"My dad and I are going home," Anne whispered.

"What?"

"Right after we pack."

"But why?" Marti sat upright.

"I'm not feeling well, and Dad wants me home,
near my own doctors."

"I thought you just had a cold."

For a moment, Anne was tempted to tell Marti the
truth, then her courage failed. She wanted Marti to
remember her fondly, not with fear or disgust. "I
have to go."

"But what about Morgan? Have you told him?"

"You tell him for me."

Marti gripped Anne's hand. "There's something really wrong with you, isn't there?"

"Yes," Anne admitted.

Marti stifled a cry, then threw her arms around Anne. "I knew it. Morgan told me about your cut and how you acted. I decided not to ask you about it, but it's got something to do with your leaving, doesn't it? Anne, tell me."

"I can't," she said miserably.

"I'll miss you so much." Marti was starting to cry.

"I'll miss you too." Anne hugged her friend tightly.

"If it weren't for you, I'd never have realized Peter was bad for me."

"What did I do?"

"You told me to date Skip. I never would have if you hadn't encouraged me. He's the best thing that ever happened to me."

"Don't tell Peter when you're back in LA," Anne kidded. "He may come after me. You were a good friend to me too, Marti, especially when I needed one who didn't ask questions. I'll never forget you."

"Will you write me?"

"I'll write." Anne knew she'd probably have plenty of time, lying in a hospital bed. She rose, but Marti refused to release her hand. "What's wrong?"

"Oh, Anne, I just had the strangest feeling. I'm afraid I'll never see you again. I know that doesn't make any sense, but I'm scared. Promise me you'll come back next year, and I will too."

"If I'm able," Anne said, trying to sound cheerful.

"I have to go." Anne extricated her hand from Marti's and headed toward the door.

"I'll light candles for you in church every Sunday," Marti said with a quivery voice.

"*Gracias.*"

Marti began to cry. "*Vaya con Dios, Anne.* Go with God."

"I will, *te amiga,*" Anne whispered, and shut the door softly behind her.

Fifteen

❧

BACK IN NEW YORK, Anne was hospitalized immediately. Her recuperation from pneumonia was long and painful, her adjustment to AZT difficult. She had no energy and was nauseous and sick. She suffered with unbearable itching. Everything made her depressed. "I can't blame it all on the AZT," she told her father. "How else is a person supposed to feel when she knows she'll never get well?"

Her doctors were thorough. They tried her on different combinations of drugs, but her T-cell count continued to plunge. When Anne confronted the doctors, they told her she now had full-blown AIDS. She took the news as courageously as possible—mostly for her father's sake.

After her release from the hospital, her father took her home where she was too weak and ill to resume a normal life. Anne was lonely. She hadn't confided in any of her friends so no one visited or called.

"Let me talk to the kids you know," her father urged.

"It doesn't matter," Anne told him, even though, deep down it did matter. She figured none of them would know what to say to her, or how to act around someone who was terminally ill. As summer faded into fall, confined to her bed in their apartment, Anne fought to keep her spirits up by reliving her Colorado summer in her daydreams.

She gazed longingly out of the window in her bedroom, watching the bare branches of a tree bend in a raw, November wind. "Can I get you anything before I head out to class?" her father asked, entering her room.

"I'm fine. You go on." She knew he hated leaving her alone.

"Mrs. Hankins must have been delayed in traffic," he added. "I can call and have someone cover my classes for me."

"Dad, she'll be here. Stop worrying."

He bent and kissed Anne's cheek. She held her breath, knowing it was a silly thing to do. She knew AIDS wasn't contagious by kissing this way, but she was nervous anyway.

"There's a PBS special on tonight," her father said. "I thought we could watch it together."

"I'd like that."

"It's a date then. I'm off for now."

"Have mercy on your poor students."

From the doorway, his smile looked tight. "Mercy. I've forgotten about that concept."

Anne adjusted the pillows against her back and sighed heavily. If only the days weren't so long. She knew JWC, her secret benefactor, understood what she was experiencing. She knew the words in the letter by heart. *"Through no fault of our own we have endured pain and isolation and have spent many days in a hospital feeling lonely and scared."* Surely, Anne decided, JWC had endured AIDS, for no one who hadn't could possibly understand. However, "lonely and scared" didn't begin to define what Anne had feared most in the hospital.

After weeks of treatment, she'd grabbed her father's hand one night and sobbed, "Promise me, you won't let me die in this place."

"Honey, you're not going to die yet," her father managed to reply.

"It's not the dying. It's the thought of dying *here.* Take me home. Please. No matter how bad it gets, promise me, you won't make me come back to the hospital."

"I can't make such a promise. I couldn't save you at home."

"Don't try. Just let me go. Don't let them hook me up to machines and keep me alive just to endure more pain." She felt desperate. "I want to go home. I want to be in my home . . . my room when it happens, Daddy."

He tried to calm her. "Take it easy. Don't think about this now. Think about getting well. I'll find out all that I can about caring for someone with AIDS at home."

"You wouldn't mind taking care of me?"

"Oh, Anne ... I won't leave you in the care of strangers. I love you."

Anne smiled at her father's tenderness. She'd met AIDS patients in the hospital who'd been disowned and abandoned by their families after their diagnosis. She couldn't understand such misery. Her father had cared enough about her to undertake the chore of home care, and devoted all of his time to her.

"Anne, it's me, Mrs. Hankins." The older woman's voice floated down the hall into Anne's room.

"I'm in my room," Anne called.

Mrs. Hankins bustled into the room. "Sorry I'm late. Missed my bus." She set down her things and took off her coat. "All ready for that bath? I thought we could wash your hair today too."

Anne was more than ready. Ever since her skin had erupted in painful, itchy shingles, her relief came from the oatmeal bath soaks Mrs. Hankins helped her with three times a week. Her hair was a different matter. Most of it had fallen out because of the drugs. She'd cut it until it was no more than a few inches long all over her head.

"Joan of Arc was also closely cropped," her father had kidded. Yet, she'd seen sorrow in his eyes when he'd gathered up the handfuls of her once long, beautiful, brown hair.

Mrs. Hankins brought out a pale pink flannel nightgown from Anne's bureau. "This is pretty. I'll help you into it when we're finished."

As Anne soaked in the soothing tub of water, Mrs. Hankins changed the bed linen and put a bouquet of fresh flowers into a vase. Anne was grateful to this woman who came several times a week to help her.

She was from a group of volunteers called Good Samaritan. Their mission was to provide practical support for AIDS patients.

"Why would you want to help me? You don't even know me." Anne had said when the chaplain at the hospital had first introduced Anne to Mrs. Hankins.

The woman's blue eyes studied her tenderly. "I lost a son, Todd, to AIDS. His own father wanted nothing to do with him. I nursed Todd, trying to ease his physical and emotional pain.

"The Good Samaritan group showed us both how to accept what had happened. To accept God's love and to forgive ourselves, and others, for what we can't change. I promised that once Todd was gone, I would continue to live out the call to love and service. It seems the very least I can do."

In the two months Mrs. Hankins had been coming to her home, Anne had become deeply connected to the caring woman who helped with her most personal needs. Her presence gave Anne's father a break from the constant strain of caregiving. There were others who helped too—a social worker, a nurse, and her doctors—but Anne appreciated Mrs. Hankins the most.

"All through?" Mrs. Hankins asked, coming into the bathroom. "Let's blow dry your hair. Would you like to put on some makeup?"

"You know none of that will help the way I look," Anne replied, refusing to so much as glance at her reflection in the mirror.

"Trust me," Mrs. Hankins said with a gleam in her eye, "it will help you feel better."

When Anne was safely tucked between clean

sheets, Mrs. Hankins said, "I'll go tidy up the kitchen."

"You don't have to do that. Dad will—"

"Your dad's a fine man, and I'm sure he's a fine professor, but his kitchen skills are a bit lacking."

Anne smiled. She was familiar with her father's bad habits. Depression stole over her as she imagined him living alone, without her. Anne struggled against it. She leaned back against the pillows and, while Mrs. Hankins bustled about the apartment, Anne stared up at the solitary patch of grey sky.

She closed her eyes and pictured the rugged mountains of Colorado etched against the bright blue heavens. The image of Morgan astride his big bay stallion galloped across the canvas of her memory. It was Morgan she missed most of all. She told herself that just as there was no more bay horse, she had no hope of ever seeing Morgan again. Yet, like the bitter wind that surged outside her window, the memories persisted, filling her with both longing and despair for what could never be.

Sixteen

❧

"PEOPLE ARE CRUEL." Over the months, Anne's words returned to Morgan time and again. What he heard her *really* say was *"You're cruel."*

The look of horror in her brown eyes and the revulsion her face expressed when he shot the bay, hounded him. She hadn't understood, of course. She'd thought him cruel and heartless, when in reality he'd done the most humane thing possible. They had parted in anger, she had left for New York, and he'd never been able to tell her he was sorry.

When Marti had first told him that Anne had gone without so much as a good-bye to him, Morgan had been furious. He couldn't believe that she'd deserted him. Marti insisted that something had been wrong with Anne, something to do with her health. Angrily, he had brushed off Marti's explanation, but as summer turned into fall and he began to overcome the hurt of Anne's abandonment, he began to remember the wonderful times they'd shared. His anger dulled, while his good memories grew vivid.

Cold November wind blasted down from the mountains, bringing snow before Thanksgiving. Skip, who'd stayed on as a regular ranch hand, took off two weeks and went to L.A. to visit Marti. Morgan tried to keep himself busy with ranch chores and with the search for a horse he liked as much as the bay.

Skip called him over Thanksgiving. "You should come out here, Morgan. The sun shines every day."

"Don't get a sunburn."

"And Hollywood is something else!"

Morgan grinned, hearing the excitement in Skip's voice. "Don't go getting 'discovered'—we need you back here. How's Marti?"

"Great. She's already asked Maggie for a job next summer. I guess I'm irresistible."

"I won't tell her you said that. Has Marti heard anything from Anne?" he asked, more casually than he felt.

"The last letter she got, Anne wrote that she'd been in the hospital, but that she was home now."

"The hospital?" Morgan felt his heart constrict. "What was wrong with her?"

"Anne never says, but Marti believes it's something really serious. Why don't you write Anne?"

"I'll think about it." Morgan hung up and thought about little else. Why was life treating him so unfairly? First his father, now Anne, and eventually, maybe even himself and Aunt Maggie. Morgan hated the injustice of it all.

A week before Christmas, he went to talk to his aunt. "I've been thinking of taking some time off," he said.

Maggie put down her pen and closed the ledger book she was working with. "You're not a hired hand, Morgan. You're family. You work hard, and if you want to get away for a while, go on."

"You don't think Uncle Don will mind?"

"If you'd gone to college, you wouldn't be here at all. He won't mind. Where will you go?"

"East." His plan had been forming for weeks, and now it had taken on an urgency.

"How long?"

"I don't know."

"I wish I could help you be happier, Morgan. Maybe some time away from here will do you good."

"It's not just that," Morgan said haltingly. "There are a lot of things I need to figure out. I need some time to sort through them."

"You know I understand."

He knew that his aunt did. She might be facing the same horrifying future as he. "I'll let you know when I get where I'm going," Morgan promised.

"This is your home, so take a break, then come back." She hugged him tight.

"Thanks, Aunt Maggie." Morgan felt a knot lodge in his throat. It was difficult to think about leaving, but he knew he must. He had to find some answers, not only about Anne Wingate, but about Morgan Lancaster too.

Anne propped herself up in bed and tried to read. The type on the page of the book kept blurring. This new problem frightened her very much. She couldn't stand the thought of losing her eyesight and not being able to read. Her father had brought her a tape recorder and stacks of books on tape, but going blind was horrifying.

Exasperated, she tossed the book aside. Out the window, the sky promised snow. Maybe they'd have a white Christmas. She smelled the scent of gingerbread coming from the kitchen. Mrs. Hankins's work, Anne knew. Her father was out doing errands. Anne had asked him not to bother with presents for her this year, but he'd been so appalled that she'd not mentioned it a second time. Still, she knew that her time was running out and hadn't wanted him to waste time and money for a Christmas she might not live to see.

Every day, she was weaker, sicker. Her latest blood work had shown a very low platelet and white blood count. Right before Thanksgiving, she'd had to return to the hospital because of a persistent cough and high fever. Thankfully, she hadn't developed pneumonia again. She heard the door buzzer; Mrs. Hankins answered it.

Minutes later, Mrs. Hankins came to Anne's room. "There's someone to see you," she said.

"To see me? Who is it?"

"A very handsome young man. He wouldn't give his name."

"He must have the wrong Anne Wingate." She couldn't imagine that anyone from school would just drop by. "I really don't feel like having visitors anyway."

"He said I had to persuade you. I told him I'd try, but it's up to you, Anne."

Anne was mystified. "What does he look like?"

"A cowboy."

Anne's stomach lurched, and her heart wedged in her throat. It couldn't be. . . . "Please don't let him in."

"I'm in." Morgan stood at the doorway.

Anne covered her face and attempted to hunch down under the covers. "Don't look at me," she cried.

"You'd better wait by the entry door," Mrs. Hankins said.

Morgan stepped around Mrs. Hankins and moved close to Anne's bed. "Look at me," he said. She kept her hands over her face, but he noticed lesions along her neck and on one of her hands.

"Go away! Please! Don't look at me! Why are you here?"

"I had to see you."

"No!" The word sounded final and tortured. "I'm hideous, I'm sick. Go away!"

"Please, young man," Mrs. Hankins said. "You're upsetting her."

Morgan gently took hold of both Anne's wrists. Even though she tried to hide, he saw her face. She looked thin and gaunt. "I let you look at me when that bronc rearranged my face last summer."

Slowly, Anne raised her eyes to meet his. She could hardly keep from weeping. She wanted to run and hide, and yet she wanted to throw her arms around him. He looked so wonderful, so healthy.

"I've changed, haven't I?" Anne asked, her voice quivering.

She'd changed horribly, he thought, but he knew what courage it had taken for her to face him. "What's wrong, Anne? We're all worried about you."

"I'm ill." She held her head higher now, almost defiantly.

"Are you allowing him to stay?" Mrs. Hankins asked.

The damage was done. There was no use trying to hide the truth from Morgan any longer. "It's all right, Mrs. Hankins. He can stay here."

"Anne tires easily," Mrs. Hankins warned. "I'll be in the kitchen, Anne."

"I want to know what's wrong with you," Morgan insisted gently once he and Anne were alone. "Please tell me. Maybe I can help."

She gestured to one of the lesions. "This is Kaposi's sarcoma. A type of skin cancer."

His gaze barely brushed over the ugly lesions. "Skin cancer is the reason you left so suddenly last summer? I want to know why you went without even saying good-bye to me."

"You should have phoned. We could have discussed it over the phone."

"Too impersonal."

"You should have told me you were coming."

"I was afraid you wouldn't see me."

"You would have been right." She sighed and nervously brushed her hand through her wispy hair. If only she could look pretty again.

"You've changed the subject," he said. "Tell me what's going on."

She hated to, feared the look of revulsion that would cross his face. "I have AIDS." She stared straight at him, waiting for him to bolt toward the door.

He felt as if he'd been slammed on the ground from the back of a bucking horse. He didn't know a lot about AIDS, but he knew it was fatal. "Is that what you've been afraid to tell me?"

"Aren't *you* afraid?" She couldn't believe he was enlightened enough not to be fearful.

Morgan shook his head. "I'm one person who isn't afraid."

It was her turn to be surprised. "Do you know someone with AIDS? Do you have AIDS?"

"No."

"Then why—"

He folded his hands together and silenced her with an anguished look. Quietly, he asked, "Have you ever heard of the disease Huntington's chorea?"

Seventeen

~~

"HUNTINGTON'S CHOREA?" ANNE searched her memory for the meaning of the name. "No, I haven't. Tell me about it."

"It's a genetic disorder. It gets passed along through families. The word 'chorea' comes from a word that means dance." Morgan gave a bitter chuckle. "It's a dance, all right. A victim has no control over his movements. For no reason, he jerks spasmodically. He gets worse and worse until he can't walk. Then his muscles get stiff and rigid. All the while, the mind is affected too, and the victim turns paranoid. Eventually, the person becomes totally disabled, no more than a living vegetable. And finally—sometimes after years of suffering—he dies of choking to death, or from pneumonia, or heart failure or a blood clot. The folk singer Woody Guthrie died of it."

Anne blinked, feeling the anguish of Morgan's description. "Why are you telling me this?"

"Do you remember when I told you that my father was dead?" Anne nodded. "That's not true," he said. "He's in an institution in St. Louis that specializes in caring for people with Huntington's."

"Oh, Morgan . . ." Anne felt tears well in her eyes.

"It's simpler to say he's dead. . . . I mean, he may as well be. He's totally disabled and out of it. I was eight when his symptoms first started, but I still remember what it was like—what he turned into. Up till then, my daddy was a big, fun-loving cowboy. One day, his body started making weird twitching motions. He started falling down while walking. At first, the doctor thought he'd had a seizure, so he put him on medicine. It didn't help.

"Then, gradually, Dad turned mean and crazy. He chased Mom with a butcher knife one time. Another time, he drove the car right through the side of the house. Finally, after five years of living with this wild, spastic lunatic, Mom and Aunt Maggie decided to lock him away. That's when another group of doctors realized he had Huntington's disease."

"Is that why your mom left?"

"When the diagnosis finally came in, she was burned out. Like I told you, Mom was once a pretty party girl. She never signed on for Huntington's."

"But she had you to care for."

"I was better off with Aunt Maggie and Uncle Don. I know it's hard to believe, but I understood why my mom left, and I didn't hold it against her. I still don't and I never will. I've made my peace with that."

Anne could hardly absorb why he wouldn't have resented her for leaving him. "But once your father was being cared for, the two of you could have made it."

"I'm not so sure." Morgan stared down at his hands. "Huntington's doesn't strike when people are real young—people get it when they're in their thirties, or even their fifties. A person—a blood relative, that is—has a fifty-fifty chance of getting it if the gene for it is already in the family."

His voice had dropped so low that Anne had to lean forward to catch the last. A silence fell in the room, and she waited for him to resume. He didn't, but in the lengthening silence, she caught the drift of what he'd left unsaid. The weight of it took the breath from her. "Your Aunt Maggie could get it," Anne said slowly. "Or you."

"That's right—either one of us. We're walking time bombs. I know Mom couldn't have faced it again. It was easier for her to walk away from the pain of the past and make sure she didn't have to face it again."

Anne couldn't understand such a solution, but she didn't say anything. She knew his aunt and uncle truly cared for him. "Isn't there any way to know if you'll get it or not?"

He shrugged and didn't answer. "When Aunt Maggie took my daddy to that nursing home, the doctors explained that it could take him upward of twenty years to die, because in other ways, he was in good health. Twenty years of existing in hell, while his brain slowly turns to jelly. Aunt Maggie and Mom got out of there as fast as they could."

"You haven't seen him in all these years?"

"No, and I don't want to." His tone sounded so fi nal. Anne wanted to tell him that if she could see her mother again, even for a minute, she wouldn't care about the circumstances, but she let Morgan continue. "I was twelve when Dad was institutional-ized, and I've lived these past six years knowing that it might happen to me . . . and that there's nothing medical science can do to stop it. There's no cure."

"I overheard your uncle say you had a death wish. At least, now I understand why."

"Maybe he's right. I guess it's easier to take chances with my life, to feel like I'm in control somehow, than to sit and wait for Huntington's cho-rea to drop in on me."

Anne comprehended his reasoning perfectly. Hadn't that been what she'd done by choosing not to begin AZT treatments when she could have, but instead going to the ranch? "It may not happen to you," Anne suggested. "You might not be doomed, and you should try not to ruin your life."

"I've got a possible twenty-year wait before I find out, and I don't want to be tested and know for sure. What kind of life is that? What kind of plans can a person make with that hanging over his head?"

"Oh, Morgan—"

"Don't feel sorry for me." He glanced at her sharply. His expression softened. "I guess I shouldn't complain so. You're the one who's worse off. Anne, you should have said something to me before you left—I care about you, about what's happening to you."

"I didn't know what to say," she replied. "Do you

think it's easy to tell someone such a dreadful thing? I wasn't sure how you'd take it. I didn't know about your problem. You didn't confide in me either."

"I guess you're right," he said. "We were both afraid."

"How did you get here anyway?" she asked, changing the subject.

"I sold the saddle." She nodded in understanding. "I never did find a horse I liked as well as the bay. Maybe something will come in off the range in the spring—a colt, something younger, easier to work with . . . not so spooky."

Anne remembered the beautiful Colorado mountains and longed for her lost summer. If only . . . "I hope so."

Morgan tried to hold on to his new feelings. He felt comfortable being with Anne. He'd never told anyone his secret until now. The intense empathy on her face touched him. Even in her pain, she could feel compassion and concern for him. He wanted to hold her, and yet, he wasn't sure she'd let him. He wasn't afraid of her AIDS. He didn't even care how she'd contracted it. All that mattered was being with her.

Feeling lost for words, he glanced around her room. It looked homey and peaceful, filled with books and posters, a stereo, and stacks of CDs. "I thought a rich girl like you would have all kinds of maids and servants," he remarked.

"You keep accusing me of being wealthy," Anne said, baffled. "Why is that?" My dad and I aren't rolling in money."

"I know how much it costs to spend a whole summer at the Broken Arrow, and how much that saddle cost. I just assumed . . ."

"Let me show you something, cowboy," she said. "I've shared my one big secret, but I have another incredible one." She reached over to her bedside table, picked up a piece of folded paper, and handed it to him. "Believe it or not, this is the source of all my wealth."

Morgan could tell the letter had been folded and refolded many times. He read, growing more astonished with every word. "You mean somebody just handed you a check for one hundred thousand dollars?" he asked when he was finished.

"Yes."

"That's hard to believe."

"It was for me too. Dad didn't want to, but I used that money for us to go out West. Even though I don't know the identity of JWC, I've been grateful for what he or she did for me. I'm positive this JWC has had a similar experience. We're kindred spirits."

"What about the rest of the money?"

"It's going to care for me while I'm sick. The medications are expensive, and the hospitalizations too."

"The woman who opened the door?"

"Actually, she's a volunteer. She lost a son to AIDS, and now she wants to help others. I've made my dad promise not to let me die stuck in the hospital," Anne explained.

"But, what if—" Morgan blurted, wishing he'd thought before he'd spoken.

"What if I get so sick, I die at home?" Anne finished his question. "That's my goal. I want to die in my own bed, with no machines or impersonal surroundings."

His eyes grew wide. "It's that control stuff again, Morgan. I can't stop myself from dying, so I'm choosing my place and my way. It was hard to convince my dad. It's not much, but it's all I have." .

Morgan stayed for dinner that night. With effort, Anne came to the dining room table, where she, Morgan, and her father ate and made small talk. All through the meal, Morgan sensed an undercurrent of hostility coming from Anne's father. After Anne was tucked into bed, he decided to talk to Dr. Wingate before he left.

Morgan approached him in the living room. "Can I speak to you, sir?"

"What is it?"

"I would like your permission to stay here in New York and to visit Anne regularly.

Dr. Wingate tapped his fingers and gave Morgan a skeptical, searching look. "Why?"

"I care about her."

"I care about her too. I don't want her hurt."

"I don't plan to hurt her."

"She's going to die, Morgan. We don't know how much longer she has, but it could take months."

"I don't care how long it takes. I want to stay."

Dr. Wingate paused, thinking. "Look, I've attended classes about how to properly care for Anne at home. We have a team of doctors involved, and volunteers too. There are precautions that must be taken every step of the way."

"I'm not afraid of catching AIDS."

"The precautions aren't for your sake. They're for hers. She's vulnerable to infections. Even a common cold could kill her, and we just made it by after her bout with pneumonia."

"I'll do whatever you want. I'd just like your permission."

"I know she likes having you here. She's shown more spirit, more spark today than she has in the last month. I won't lie to you—these past few months have been pretty hard on me. I attend a support group for parents." He adjusted his glasses and stared hard at Morgan. "If you want to stay, I won't stop you. If you can make my daughter's life better, I can make room for you here in the apartment."

"Look, I don't want to put you out. Maybe I can find a place—"

"This is New York City, Morgan, not Colorado. You don't want to be in some fleabag hotel. No . . . you'll be better off here—if you want to be."

Morgan thought his offer sounded almost like a challenge. "All right," Morgan said. "I'll move in. Thank you."

"You may not thank me for long, Morgan. I'm doing this for my daughter. Whatever time she's got left, I want her to be happy. You make her happy. Please, don't do anything to hurt her. She's suffering enough already. She got AIDS through a blood transfusion that we thought would save her life. Now, no one can save her."

Eighteen

༺༻

MORGAN READ EVERYTHING Anne's father gave him about AIDS. The facts made him shudder. What a terrible way for a person to die, he thought. About as terrible as having Huntington's chorea. "The real enemy is death," Anne told him during one of their many long talks. "Sometimes when I hurt really bad, I think of death as a friend, but then I think about how wonderful it is to be alive, and I see death as terrible. I wish I could live. There's so much I wanted to do."

He reached over and took her hand. If death was her enemy, he wanted to hold it off for her. "I've been wanting to ask you something."

She clung to his hand. His skin was warm, and it felt so good to be touched. These days, few people touched her without wearing latex gloves. "Ask me before the pain pill takes effect and I get spacey," she said.

"The night I asked you to stay with me . . . would you have stayed if it hadn't been for HIV?"

She thought for a long time before answering. "I know this is going to sound corny, but I'm going to say it anyway. That night, I wanted to stay. But deep down inside, I've always wanted to wear white at my wedding and have it mean something. Not that I've ever longed to get married," she added hastily. "I always wanted other things first. College, of course. A career. But *if*—and this is a big if—I ever was to get married, I'd want my husband to be the first man and the only man."

"It doesn't sound corny."

"Knowing that I could have infected you with HIV made me know to stop. Still, I want to believe that even if I hadn't been HIV-positive, I would have said no. It's nice to think that you can do something noble, even when it goes against what you want to do." She touched his cheek, "Morgan, I *was* tempted."

He smiled ruefully. "I wanted you to stay, but in a way, I was glad you didn't. Even though the rejection hurt, it made you more special."

She fell asleep smiling. Morgan watched her, reliving the short time they'd shared in Colorado. The night he'd held her, almost made love to her . . . the afternoon in the old church and cemetery . . . the picnic in the field of flowers . . .

Looking at her now, he saw beyond the gauntness, beyond the skin eruptions, the shorn hair, the pallor of her flesh. What he saw was a girl he loved and could never, ever have.

*   *   *

On Christmas Day, Anne's father carried her out to the tree in the living room. He settled her gently on the sofa and proceeded to heap her lap full of gifts. "Dad, you shouldn't have," she protested.

"Hey, it's Christmas. You know I couldn't let it pass without buying you my usual assortment of useless presents!"

She struggled with the wrappings. He knelt on the floor in front of her. He reminded Morgan of a little kid trying hard to please. "Here, let me help. I told that clerk not to use so much tape."

She opened boxes packed with sweaters, socks, a fleece bathrobe, sets of pajamas, and classical music CDs. "It's too much, Dad," she admonished.

"I saved the best for last," he said, pulling out one more small, flat box.

She opened it and let out a delighted cry. "Daddy, it's a first-edition Emily Dickinson! You shouldn't have! I love it. It's beautiful." She held up the book and flipped through it, eyes glowing. She leaned down and hugged him.

"I did a computer search and found it in an antiquarian bookstore in Boston."

Anne showed the book to Morgan. "Give my dad that box with the red paper, please" she said. "I've got something extra special for you too, Dad."

Morgan fetched it, and Anne's father shook it dutifully. "It's heavy."

"Be careful with that."

He undid the box. Inside lay a hinged photo frame, and when he swung it open, tears formed in his eyes. On one side was a photo of Anne's mother;

on the other, a photo of Anne. Morgan, looking over Dr. Wingate's shoulder, couldn't believe the resemblance between the two women. "Mrs. Hankins helped me," Anne said, seeing her father's reaction. "I slipped your favorite one of Mom—the one that got damaged years ago—from the album and had it restored and hand-colored. The one of me was my sophomore yearbook photo."

"You told me they weren't any good."

"Well, I changed my mind. I mean, considering the way I look now."

He looked up at her and held the photos to his chest. "You're beautiful," he whispered. "You're both beautiful, and I'll treasure this forever."

Morgan felt awkward, as if he was intruding. "I got you something too," Anne told Morgan. "Mrs. Hankins selected it, but I told her what to get."

Morgan ripped open the box to find a heavy sweater of dark navy blue, along with a framed photo of Anne on Golden Star.

"Marti took it this summer and sent me the negative. I had it enlarged."

He couldn't take his eyes from it. She looked lovely and perfectly healthy. "Thank you," was all he could manage.

"It was one of the best times of my life," she said. "I'll always be glad I went."

"Aunt Maggie shipped this to me for you." He fished around under the tree and dragged out the gift he had for Anne. He wanted Anne to like it, hoped she'd grasp what he really wanted to tell her, but couldn't put into words.

She removed the paper slowly, with effort, because her hands ached so badly. Inside the box lay a pale buckskin dress, adorned with beads and feathers. "Remember, I told you that my great-great-great grandmother was a full-blooded Cheyenne?" Morgan asked.

The afternoon in the cemetery by the church sprang vividly into Anne's mind. "I remember."

"That's a Cheyenne ceremonial wedding dress. I thought you might like to see what one looks like."

She placed the soft deerskin against her cheek. She understood what he meant through the gift, what he couldn't say in front of her father. A large lump swelled her throat shut as she gazed into the depths of his blue eyes. "The Cheyenne must have been wonderful people," she said softly, "to have dressed their brides in such splendor."

He wished he could tell her how special he thought she was. He wanted to thank her for allowing him into her life. He wanted to tell her that this was the best Christmas he'd known in years. "Cheyenne women are brave and beautiful," he replied. "And I should know."

Anne's father served turkey with all the trimmings. Morgan ate heartily, to make up in part for Anne's eating almost nothing. Afterward, he insisted she call Marti, who squealed with delight when she heard Anne's voice. "*Feliz Navidad*," Marti shouted.

Hearing Marti's voice triggered a flood of memories. "Morgan tells me you're going back to the ranch next summer," Anne said.

"Oh, Anne, if only you could come back too."

If only . . . "I'll be with you in spirit."

"I'm glad Morgan's with you," Marti said, her tone subdued. "I *told* you he liked you."

"Have a wonderful life, Marti."

"*Te amo*, Anne."

"I love you too." Anne hung up and wept softly. There were so many people she was going to miss.

"I didn't want you to be sad," Morgan said, apologetically.

"It's all right. I'm glad I talked to her. You make sure Skip treats her right. Her old boyfriend didn't. She deserves the best."

Toward nightfall, Morgan went for a long walk alone. Snow had fallen, fresh and white, but had turned dingy in the streets. Everywhere he turned, there was traffic, noise, and people hurrying along the sidewalks. He began to miss the solitude and beauty of Colorado. Yet, he'd promised himself he would stay for as long as Anne was alive. He thought about trying to find a job, something to help Anne's father with expenses. He wanted to contribute in some way.

By the time he returned to the apartment, it was late. Certain Anne was asleep, Morgan crept toward his sleeper sofa. A light coming from Dr. Wingate's study caught his eye. He wondered why Anne's father would be working on Christmas night, then decided to talk to him about getting work. Morgan tapped on the door, and entered after hearing a muffled, "Come in."

He saw Anne sitting in front of her father's computer. Surprised, Morgan blurted, "What are you doing up so late?"

She gave him a weary smile and gestured toward

an empty chair beside the desk. "I've been touring various libraries," she said.

"What?"

Anne tapped several computer keys, and the printer began clacking. "My father gave me the idea when he told me how he searched for the Emily Dickinson book. I don't know why I didn't think of it before."

"Think of what?"

"Doing a computer search about Huntington's chorea," she said. "Sit down. I've discovered some very interesting information for you."

Nineteen

⁓

MORGAN WENT HOT and cold all over. He wasn't sure he wanted any more information about Huntington's. "You should be resting," he told Anne. "It isn't good for you to be up this late."

"I'll have an eternity to rest," she said matter-of-factly. "I only have now to be alive."

"Don't talk that way."

"Sit down," she repeated. "There are some things you need to know." He sat. She tore off paper from the printer. "I researched medical magazines and newspaper articles. I've read and printed out the material for you. The interviews with people who are facing the prospect of Huntington's are interesting."

"Let me guess," Morgan said dourly. "It's tough to make plans."

"First of all, I think you shouldn't be afraid to take the test. The test wasn't in use until 1986. I guess it's like my AIDS problem. They started screening blood in eighty-five—too late for me." She shook her head. "Anyway, the test is a predictor. It requires blood samples from your relatives, like you and your Aunt Maggie and your father. Is there anyone else in your father's family?"

"I don't think so. My grandparents died years ago."

"The test looks for certain DNA markers on genes of groups of family members. If the marker's found in any one person's genes, it means the person will get Huntington's. If it isn't, he's home free."

"I know about the test. So what?"

Amazed by his lack of interest, Anne declared, "All it takes is a blood sample, and according to reports, the test is over ninety percent accurate." She shuffled through the papers in her hand. "The testing is expensive, up to five thousand dollars, but it would settle the matter once and for all for you and your aunt."

Morgan gave her a quizzical look. "And what if the test is positive? What if it tells me I'm going to get Huntington's? I'd get to trade worrying about *if* the disease will strike for worrying about *when*. What kind of comfort is that?"

Anne was at a loss for words. She'd thought he'd be overjoyed to know he could stop living with uncertainty. "I figured you might want to know. You could prepare—"

Morgan bolted out of the chair. "Well, I don't want to know. If it's going to happen to me, then I'll have years and years to think about ending up like my father. Plenty of time to contemplate turning into a maniac and living in an institution."

"But you'd also have time to plan for your life."

"What kind of plans does a person make when he knows he's going to die a horrible death?" She stiffened, and instantly, he wished he'd minded his tongue. "I'm sorry. I didn't mean to hurt you."

"Believe me, I know what it's like to live with an automatic death sentence, Morgan. I know what it's like to feel your life slipping away from you, and know that all the medical technology in the world can't save you. But even so, you have choices. I chose to spend the summer in Colorado instead of the hospital. What I'm telling you is that you may not have to live with a death sentence. You have the opportunity to know if you can live a normal life or not."

"What's the point?"

"You don't have to take such reckless chances with your life. You don't have to keep courting death, daring it by living dangerously."

"Now you sound like my aunt and uncle."

"You can make plans for a future," Anne pleaded.

"It isn't that simple," he insisted. "If the test is positive and people find out, how do you think they'll treat me?"

Morgan had begun pacing. Suddenly, he walked over to the chair where Anne sat. "What if Aunt Maggie and I took this test, and I found out she's going to get it but I'm not? How do you think that would make me feel? Or what if it's the other way around?"

"You'd let guilt stand in the way of knowing the

truth? Truth sets people free. Don't you want to be free?"

He avoided Anne's question. "My aunt's been good to me. I don't want to see her suffer."

"Doesn't she wonder if it's going to happen to her?"

"Sure she does. She told me that every time she drops something, or trips, she wonders if it's the start of Huntington's for her." He thought a moment, then asked, "Both of us would have to take it—isn't that what your research says?"

" 'The larger the genetic sample, the more accurate the results,' " Anne quoted from one of the pages.

Morgan rocked back on his heels. "Does any of your research say there's a cure yet for Huntington's?"

"No. It's like AIDS—no cure."

"Then we're back to square one, aren't we? What's the point?"

Anne felt frustrated. Why was he being so stubborn? He was allowing his irrational fears to direct the course of his life. "So, you don't want to know? You don't want to ever take the test?"

Morgan leaned down over her chair. "So long as I don't know, I have hope it won't strike me. Without hope, what else is there?"

"That's not hope—that's gambling, playing the odds." She reached up and touched his cheek. "I knew that I had no hope of living—of beating AIDS. But it didn't keep me from wanting to live every moment I had left. If I hadn't wanted that, I would never have met you."

Morgan felt a heaviness in his chest. He wanted to

hit something with his fist. He wanted to tear something apart with his bare hands. He looked down into Anne's upturned face and forced the anger down. He pulled her to her feet and gently wrapped her thin, frail body in his arms.

She lay her cheek against his chest and felt his lips move in her hair. She heard his voice come softly from above her. "Anne, I appreciate all you've tried to do for me, all the time and energy you spent on this project. I can't face it the way you have. I wish I could, but I can't. Please understand."

She clung to him fiercely. "I understand," she whispered sadly, knowing that she didn't.

Christmas was the last good day Anne remembered having. She ran a fever which rose steadily, and began to cough. The home-care nurse listened to her lungs. "She should be in the hospital," the nurse told Anne's father.

Racked with pain, Anne turned glazed eyes toward him. "No hospital," she wheezed. "You promised. It's my choice."

Her father's face looked ashen and tortured. "Isn't there anything we can do for her at home?"

"Oxygen, of course," the nurse said in resignation.

A portable tank was brought in, and a mask slipped over Anne's mouth and nose. More medications were ordered, and an IV was inserted into her arm to maintain proper nutrition. She slept propped up on a stack of pillows.

Morgan acted like a caged cat. He paced, went out on endless walks, but would suddenly panic, thinking that Anne had died and he hadn't been with her.

Then he'd turn and run down the sidewalk like a madman all the way back to the apartment. Heart pounding, he would rush inside and to her room; only when he saw her, heard her labored breathing, would he calm himself.

He felt that there was something left unfinished between them. He couldn't determine what. He only knew their differing viewpoints about the test for Huntington's had become some sort of wedge. Anne was too ill for them to discuss it again, but he thought about it constantly. He wanted to be at peace with her, wanted her to know how much he loved her and would miss her.

One afternoon, he stole quietly into her room. Her eyes were closed, and the book of poetry her father had given her for Christmas lay across her lap. He watched her chest heave, listened to the hiss of the oxygen tank. Her eyelids fluttered open. "Hi," he said.

She smiled weakly. "Hi, yourself. I was having a dream."

"About me?"

"You're so vain. I was dreaming about my mother. I was a little girl again, and we were together." Morgan swallowed against the thick knot in his throat. "I'll see her soon," Anne continued.

"Please, don't . . ."

"No tears in heaven, Morgan. Remember that."

He turned his head, not wanting her to see the tears in his eyes. He took a long, shuddering breath. "Were you reading?" he asked, pointing to the book.

"Trying to. My vision keeps blurring. Very annoying. I know most of her poems by heart anyway, so I guess it shouldn't matter."

He picked up the book and dragged a stool beside her bed. "Want me to read to you?"

"You told me you don't like to read."

"I don't mind." He leaned forward. "Just don't tell Skip!"

"Your secret's safe with me."

He thumped through the slim volume of verses. "I forgot how depressing Emily was."

"A poet par excellence," Anne said. The effort cost her, but she felt a sense of peace come over her. How wonderful it was to have Morgan holding her book, doing this kindness for her that went against his rugged nature.

"Which poem?" he asked.

"You choose," she said.

He flipped a few more pages, then settled on the one he knew she liked best. In his deep, voice, he read, " 'Because I could not stop for Death— / He kindly stopped for me— / The Carriage held but just Ourselves— / And Immortality. . . . ' "

Twenty

"ANNE, ANNE!" MORGAN was awakened from a sound sleep by the voice of Anne's father shouting her name. Morgan rushed to Anne's room. Dr. Wingate was frantically trying to get her to respond, desperately trying to find a pulse. "Call nine-one-one!" he yelled at Morgan.

The emergency squad arrived in minutes, and although the team tried to resuscitate her, they couldn't. Morgan hung in the hall, feeling numb and cold. He couldn't see her body for all the people surrounding her bed. He didn't want to, really. He wanted to remember Anne as she'd been in life, with a smile on her lips, her eyes closed, listening to him read her favorite poetry. Death had come for Anne Wingate. Morgan hoped that her final journey had been painless.

Once the body had been taken away, Dr. Wingate

sat on the sofa and stared at the floor with red-rimmed eyes. Morgan called Mrs. Hankins and told her. "Oh, my poor, dear girl," she cried. "I'd come to love her like a daughter." The older woman sniffed and added, "It was a merciful way for her to die, you know . . . to simply slip away into heaven in her sleep. I've seen AIDS patients die much more horribly."

Morgan took little comfort in her words. Anne was gone. Nothing could bring her back. "Dr. Wingate wants to have a memorial service here after Anne's funeral," Morgan said. "He wants all the people who cared for her to come here instead of to the cemetery."

"I'll make some calls," Mrs. Hankins offered. "You make sure the professor takes care of himself."

Over the next two days, Morgan and Anne's father worked silently, side by side, taking care of necessary arrangements. They dressed Anne in the Cheyenne wedding dress. She looked beautiful lying on a bed of white satin, in the soft buckskin decorated with feathers and beads. In the coffin with her, Dr. Wingate placed a photo of Anne's mother and the One Last Wish letter. "It gave her so much joy," he explained to Morgan.

"Did you ever learn who JWC is?"

"No. In a way, I don't want to know. I'd like to believe that this JWC is part of life's mystery—someone who is kind and good. He or she is probably somewhere in the world doing other generous things for good people like Anne right now. It helps balance out a world where someone gets AIDS and dies before her time."

At the memorial service, Morgan realized it was comforting to sit around with the people who had known and loved Anne and hear them share memories of her. When Marti called from Los Angeles he was grateful to hear her voice.

By the end of the week, Morgan started packing his things. He folded shirts and jeans, stuffing them along with his Christmas gifts into two duffel bags. Since he hated good-byes, he'd planned to be gone before Anne's father returned from teaching his morning classes. Morgan wrote him a note and thanked him for allowing him to be a part of Anne's final weeks.

Anne's father came in just as Morgan was finishing. "I didn't expect you back so early," Morgan said.

"Today was my last class till the fall," Dr. Wingate replied. "The head of my department told me to take my sabbatical early. Anne and I were planning to visit England next summer, you know." He struggled to keep his voice even. "Anyway, they told me to go on now, so I am. I'll be going to London."

Morgan felt sorry for him. "I'm sure the time off will be good for you," he said.

"Are you leaving now?"

"I don't want to wear out my welcome."

"You won't, Morgan." The tall man rested his hand on Morgan's shoulder. "I know I didn't exactly welcome you here with open arms when you first came, but I'm glad you've been here. I truly appreciate all you gave to my Anne."

"Thank you, sir."

"Anne was very fond of you. You made the time she had left special. I'll always be grateful."

Morgan swallowed against the thick lump in his throat. So far, he'd kept his tears private, and he didn't want to lose it now. "I'll never forget her."

"Are you going back to Colorado?"

"Not directly. I have a stopover to make in St. Louis. Someone I need to visit."

"Family?" Morgan nodded. "You're lucky," Dr. Wingate said with a sad smile. "I wish I had more family around me. I wish . . ." He shook his head and tried to collect himself. "I feel so lost, even though I tried to prepare myself for the inevitable!"

"You're entitled." Morgan picked up his bags.

"Wait." Anne's father said. "Anne gave me something to give to you." He patted his pockets. "It's here, I know. She wanted to be sure you got it. Here it is."

Morgan took the white envelope carefully.

Dr. Wingate explained, "I know that it's a check. Anne told me it was for some expensive test that you might want to take someday. A test you need to take. You know, Morgan, Anne's right—you should really think about going on to college. From what I know, you're a bright young man, and it's not as if I don't see plenty of freshmen entering college. Trust my judgment. Don't waste your life."

Morgan stared at the envelope and read what Anne had written: *"The true miracle is in giving, not receiving."* He recognized the words from her One Last Wish letter. Of course, Anne's father had no way of knowing what test Anne was talking about, but for Morgan, knowing that she'd given him the means to explore his future left him dumbstruck.

"Thank you" was the best he could trust his voice to say as he tucked the envelope into his coat pocket.

He held out his hand, and Anne's father shook it. "Keep in touch, please," Dr. Wingate said. "You know where to find me."

Morgan agreed, then heaved his bags and started down the hall. As he passed Anne's room, he stopped and stood in the doorway. His gaze swept through it. The bed was neatly made; the sickroom paraphernalia, removed. A shaft of winter sunlight poured through the window. The room looked soft and shimmery, ready and waiting for someone who would never return.

He closed his eyes and recalled Anne's face, her smile. He realized that she had been like one of the shooting stars he'd seen so often in the Colorado night sky. Anne had streaked across his life and lit up its darkness.

He caught the scent of a garden drifting from her room, but wasn't surprised. *"Daddy says one can always distinguish a great lady. The air around her smells like flowers."* Morgan heard Anne's voice as clearly as he had on the golden summer afternoon only months before. He nodded in understanding, even though he saw no flowers in her room. Her presence would always linger in his life, no matter what his future held.

"I won't forget you, Anne," he vowed. Morgan turned and walked quickly toward the front door.

ABOUT THE AUTHOR

LURLENE MCDANIEL has been a professional writer for more than twenty years and has written radio and television scripts, promotional and advertising copy, and a magazine column. She began writing inspirational novels about life-altering situations for children and young adults after one of her sons was diagnosed with juvenile diabetes. She lives in Chattanooga, Tennessee.

Lurlene McDaniel's popular Bantam Starfire books include *Too Young to Die, Goodbye Doesn't Mean Forever, Somewhere Between Life and Death, Time to Let Go, Now I Lay Me Down to Sleep, When Happily Ever After Ends,* and the other One Last Wish novels *A Time to Die, Mourning Song, Mother, Help Me Live,* and *Someone Dies, Someone Lives.*